RAW APPETITES

The scout watched as Carmella Morales approached, her hips swaying in a tantalizing rhythm.

"I had hoped to find you, Eli," she said, her tone warm and honeyed, her posture promising things the scout never expected. "Are you interested in supper? The *El Pescador* had wonderful food. Especially the shellfish. Oysters and clams make a man proud all night, you know."

Holten's right eyebrow rose quizzically. "No, I didn't know," he answered, his heart racing. "But I'm willing to find out."

"Bueno," Carmella said and gave him a secret, knowing smile. "We will eat and then we shall see if what is said is true!"

THE NEWEST ADVENTURES AND ESCAPADES OF BOLT

by Cort Martin

#11: THE LAST BORDELLO (1224, $2.25)

A working girl in Angel's camp doesn't stand a chance—unless Jared Bolt takes up arms to bring a little peace to the town . . . and discovers that the trouble is caused by a woman who used to do the same!

#12: THE HANGTOWN HARLOTS (1274, $2.25)

When the miners come to town, the local girls are used to having wild parties, but events are turning ugly . . . and murderous. Jared Bolt knows the trade of tricking better than anyone, though, and is always the first to come to a lady in need . . .

#13: MONTANA MISTRESS (1316, $2.25)

Roland Cameron owns the local bank, the sheriff, and the town—and he thinks he owns the sensuous saloon singer, Charity, as well. But the moment Bolt and Charity eye each other there's fire—especially gunfire!

#14: VIRGINIA CITY VIRGIN (1360, $2.25)

When Katie's bawdy house holds a high stakes raffle, Bolt figures to take a chance. It's winner take all—and the prize is a budding nineteen year old virgin! But there's a passle of gun-toting folks who'd rather see Bolt in a coffin than in the virgin's bed!

#15: BORDELLO BACKSHOOTER (1411, $2.25)

Nobody has ever seen the face of curvaceous Cherry Bonner, the mysterious madam of the bawdiest bordello in Cheyenne. When Bolt keeps a pimp with big ideas and a terrible temper from having his way with Cherry, gunfire flares and a gambling man would bet on murder: Bolt's!

#16: HARDCASE HUSSY (1513, $2.25)

Traveling to set up his next bordello, Bolt is surrounded by six prime ladies of the evening. But just as Bolt is about to explore this lovely terrain, their stagecoach is ambushed by the murdering Beeler gang, bucking to be in Bolt's position!

Available wherever paperbacks are sold, or order direct from the Publisher. Send cover price plus 50¢ per copy for mailing and handling to Zebra Books, Dept. 1813, 475 Park Avenue South, New York, N.Y. 10016. DO NOT SEND CASH.

#20

THE SCOUT

BIG BAJA BOUNTY

BY BUCK GENTRY

ZEBRA BOOKS
KENSINGTON PUBLISHING CORP.

Special acknowledgements to Mark K. Roberts
for his contributions to this volume

ZEBRA BOOKS

are published by

Kensington Publishing Corp.
475 Park Avenue South
New York, NY 10016

First printing: April 1986

Printed in the United States of America

This book is dedicated to the real Iron Mike Madonna and the gallant men and women who serve with him in the United States Coast Guard. All the best.

BG

"*Almost from the first, he* [Kit Carson] *stood out among the men we engaged as scouts. By the time we reached the Sierras, all doubt had been removed. As much as any man on the expedition, Kit Carson served beyond the call of duty in opening California to American settlement.*"

—Col. John C. Freemont

"*Scouting is a congenial profession leading to a terrible death.*"

—George Armstrong Custer

Chapter 1

Poorly cast church bells flatly clanged to announce a new day in Santiago, Baja California, Mexico. Roosters had declared the same morning an hour earlier.

Now, at six o'clock, men and women began to stir about. Burros brayed stridently, demanding food and protesting the prospect of yet another hard stint of labor until dusk.

The first three strokes sounded, stopped and the second set started as thin wisps of smoke rose from red clay tile chimney pots all over the village of three hundred souls. Tendrils of fog from the small bay still hung in the streets and seemed to shimmer.

Corporal Gaston Obraras swung his bulk from the comfort of his bed, scratched his bare, hairless chest and yawned prodigiously. *Mierde!* Another day in this pesthole, he thought with disgust. He missed the bright lights and gay laughter of the capital.

Ciudad Mexico. That's where he belonged. If he hadn't gotten *borracho* and pasted that simpering sissy of a *lancero* lieutenant in the mouth for insulting his wife, he would still be a sergeant and assigned to comfortable duty at the center of the world, at the citadel of Chapultapec.

Oh, well, the rotund, seriously overweight non-com consoled himself. At least he didn't have to sleep with pigs and burros like his men.

The stable, which had been converted into the barracks for him and his men, still reeked of its former occupants. It was a tragic come-down in the world for one so sensitive to the subtle pleasures and heady atmosphere of Ciudad Mexico. The corporal's lamentations, as they did every day, continued while he dressed and tended to his morning toilet. His wife, meanwhile, prepared and brought him a cup of frothy chocolate. He had yet to slip on his uniform tunic and fasten the belt that held his sabre and holstered revolver when another bell began to make insistent intrusions on his glum reflections.

An alarm? Impossible. Why should that burro of a Lopez be ringing the harbor alarm bell?

"What is it, Gaston?" his wife inquired.

"Idiocy, Margarita. Nothing more. Still, a man must do his duty." He patted his pretty wife on her firm, ample behind and started for the door that separated their lodgings from his men's quarters.

Corporal Obraras burst into the long, low-ceilinged room, formerly occupied by burros and pigs, shouting to his men. "*Arriba!* Up! Up, you lazy louts. The alarm bell rings!"

With groans and complaints, they began to comply. Such a sorry lot! What a god-forsaken place. At least, the unhappy corporal consoled himself, he was in charge. Santiago de Baja was the end of the world, especially with only himself and these thirteen men as the sole local representatives of the military governor. Without breaking stride, Obraras paced to the far end of the barracks and threw open the wide, double doors to let in the bright, yellow morning light. A pace beyond the casement, he stopped in astonishment and stared at the sight on the bay.

A ship, *por Dios!* No . . . two. All of a sudden the two sleek, powerful-looking vessels executed a sharp echelon turn to starboard, and puffs of white smoke boomed from the dark holes of gunports along the sides. Obraras heard the hollow howls of roundshot hurtling through the air toward town before his mind could fully register the dull sounds of the cannon.

De varas, they were not firing a friendly salute! He thought of the harbor defense—one solitary cannon, ancient, rusted, the bore badly pitted. It had been abandoned by the English pirate, Coromuel, who had preyed upon these shores more than two centuries ago. Obraras doubted that it could even fire a projectile.

"Diez milliones demonios desde al inferno!" he shouted aloud.

The roundshot struck.

Bits and pieces of the native stone quay, the broad esplanade of the *melecón* and the fronts of houses along the bayfront flew high into the air. The invading ships had come full about and another broadside erupted from the ports in their waists. Closer inshore now, their hollow, bursting shot crashed into the town proper, exploding with violent results.

"Por Dios!"

"Hijo de la chingada!"

Obraras's squad came spilling out of the barracks, struggling into uniforms. Like their leader, they stopped, dumb-struck, to stare at the destruction that visited Santiago. With unexpected swiftness, the thunder of hoofs sounded from behind them, in the direction of the high road to Cabo San Lucas. Obraras turned jerkily.

"Cavalry! Mounted soldiers coming. *A armas, compañeros! A armas!*"

The soldiers scrambled to grab up their rifles. Thank the Good Lord they had been provided with the most modern of personal weapons, Gaston Obraras considered gratefully as he, too, rushed to obtain his Mondragon copy of the American Model 68 Springfield. Around him, trapdoors clattered metallicly as the men opened their breeches and chambered the smooth, brass rounds.

"Bayonettes. Don't forget bayonettes, my brave soldiers. Cavalry do not like cold steel."

A crackle of discharging carbines shivered the close air of the barracks as the charging enemy pounded nearer to the military compound. Dust filtered out of the vegas of the ceiling as heavy 405 grain slugs struck the adobe structure.

"*A punto! . . . Fuego!*" Corporal Obraras shouted over the rumble of the attackers' horses.

Three large, burly men in the lead went down, their mounts rearing and screaming in fear.

"*Carga! . . . A punto! . . . Fuego!*" Gastón ordered the next volley.

Nearer their target now, five of the pale-faced invaders flew from their saddles and flopped on the dusty yellow soil of the southern tip of Baja California. *Gringos!* Gaston Obraras could hardly believe it. It had been thirty years since the hated *Norte Americanos* had invaded Mexico. He had been only a small boy, running brown and naked in the streets of his native village of Atontonilco when that war had been fought. Could they have possibly come back?

No. These *gringos* wore no recognizable uniforms,

save for the bright red armbands on their left sides and the white plumes in the sweat-bands of their hats. Obraras knew that the time had come to break the charge or be overwhelmed.

"Outside. Form two ranks. Bayonettes at full extension. Aim upward for the horses' chests," he commanded.

His men obeyed with alacrity. They knew that death hovered but a short ways above them. They could stand and fight, and maybe be killed doing their duty. Or they could run, only to be hunted down like rats in a garbage heap. All of them had seen bandit attacks, or the aftermath of them. These men might attack like trained soldiers, but they were bandits all the same. Yes, they knew their enemy, though not his name.

So they stood their ground, while carbines cracked and sabres flashed in the air over their heads. They could smell the raw dust now, and horse sweat, and the sweet-sour odor of blood. Grim-faced, they braced for contact with the attackers.

It came with a stupendous crash.

Horses reared and plunged, shrieking pitifully as their determined riders impaled the beasts on the twenty-six inch triangular blades of Mexican bayonettes. A man in Obraras's front rank howled, dropped his rifle and clutched his nearly severed neck as he crumpled on the ground. Immediately a soldier from the rear file stepped forward to close the gap.

"*Fuego!* Fire at will," Gaston Obraras commanded over the tumult.

More cannonballs exploded in the town. Fires had started and women screamed in helpless terror. The cavalry force split and flowed around the hot contest at the low gate to the military post, leaving twenty-five men to battle the soldiers.

"When, oh God, when would it end?" Corporal Obraras wondered in desperation as he felt his bayonette break off in the thick chest of a bay gelding in front of him. He raised his rifle and clubbed the rider in the face with the buttstock. He would have to reload or die on the spot.

Self-appointed "Captain" Milo "Iron Mike" Madonna sat astride his magnificent Arabian stallion, normally restless hands dormant on the pommel of his saddle. He watched the village below from a slight rise to the west. To his right, the road to Cabo San Lucas lay dusty and crowded with advancing soldiers. A splendid army, he enthused.

More than five hundred men; infantry, cavalry and artillery. A big, powerfully built man, Iron Mike ran strong fingers through his curly blond hair and returned his attention to the fighting below in Santiago. A single squad held off twenty-five or so of his cavalry. Iron Mike nodded knowingly.

Someone of considerable skill, taking into account the average Mexican non-com, commanded those brave men. Too bad they would all die eventually. For die they would.

Spread too thin, suffering from an impossibly low budget, the few soldiers the Mexican army managed to field in Baja California could never stand against the might of the freebooter force Iron Mike had welded together. Despite the lack of the arms and munitions supposed to be provided by Myron Henshaw, Iron Mike's force of adventurers had been fitted out in a better manner than even the elite Presidential Guard in Mexico City.

When Henshaw had arrived to report his failure, Capt. Madonna had activated an alternative plan. He simply raided the west coast of small, turmoil-torn Nicaragua with a force of two hundred men and took what he wanted. His shopping list included six gallopers; two each finely cast brass four, six and eight pounders on lightweight carriages. Also a pair of long-range Napoleon twelve pounders. With them, and his piratical partner's shipboard twenty-four pounders, he could shell into submission any town of any size in all of Baja California. Henshaw had remained and now sat his nervous gelding to Madonna's left. The commander of the invading army cast a cold, blue gaze on him and wondered what real values the man had.

"It's going smoothly," Henshaw observed with a nod toward Santiago.

"Could be better," Madonna allowed. "Those soldiers down there are putting up a good defense."

Henshaw sniggered. "Wait until the gallopers get set up."

"My men would have to disengage before they can be used, and that could be costly. It would also allow the Mexicans to disperse and organize resistance on the part of the civilians. A peon with a machete can kill a cavalryman quite as dead as any soldier with a Springfield. Then there's the possibility of snipers. No, they will have to finish this hand-to-hand."

"Rather primitive, don't you think?"

"But effective and with the least loss of lives on our side. I didn't notice your tactics being so brilliant when it came to obtaining ordnance for this venture."

Madonna's insult stung. Myron Henshaw scowled and made as though to speak, but thought better of it. Instead he pointed to the fires burning within the town.

"I see. Shipboard gunnery is not all that accurate. Particularly with an undisciplined crew of pirates." Madonna sighed in resignation. "What they lack in finesse, they make up in ferocity. Once we've taken this town, the plundering will be terrible to behold."

A shout went up from the attacking freebooters as the last Mexican soldier fell, wounded or dead, and the main force rushed into Santiago. Iron Mike's prediction proved only too true when the final resistance broke and the frigates in the harbor disgourged their landing parties.

Soldiers and pirates met in the streets and began a systematic looting of buildings, corpses, and the terrified residents of the small town. Women screamed as burly adventurers and wiry buccaneers dragged them off to all sides of the plaza to be raped. More fires broke out and every available drop of potable liquor ran down the gullets of the conquerors. Left behind by the invaders, Corporal Obraras roused himself, and felt the throbbing wound across his forehead, over his right eye.

He had been lucky. A steel buttplate had cut his scalp and made the slight wound appear more devastating than it had in fact been. The force behind that blow had knocked him unconscious and the *gringos* had gone on, thinking him dead. Gingerly he tried his extremities, then, head spinning, pulled himself to hands and knees. He retrieved his Mondragon rifle and began to crawl toward the central plaza.

They had lost. Of that much he could be sure. That

what he intended now would surely guarantee he would die, he also accepted. All the same, his duty demanded it.

His honor demanded it.

More importantly, his *machismo* demanded it.

Obraras paused to wipe blood from his left eye. His senses pulsed, in-out, in-out, with each throb of his laboring heart. He felt bits of gravel and stucco bite through his trousers and into the tender flesh of his knees. It could not be helped. His difficult final journey consumed half an hour more and he heard the first three peals of the noon-time church bells sounding the *Angelus.* How sweetly fitting, his swimming mind suggested.

Three more flat notes resounded in the plaza. There, near the fountain. An *hombre muy importante.* One of the leaders. With supreme effort, Gaston Obraras raised his rifle and sighted on Iron Mike Madonna. No one noticed him in his hidden spot as he pulled back the long hammer and started to squeeze on the trigger.

A woman screamed. She pleaded, her voice completely familiar to Gaston Obraras. *Dios mio!* His wife. A tattooed pirate dragged her by one arm and her hair toward a recess under the stairs to the balcony of the alcalde's residence on the plaza.

Rape.

The word and the deed it described enflamed Gaston's brain. He jerked the long barrel of his Mandragon rifle off his intended target and lined up on the seaman. Flame and smoke belched from the muzzle of the .45-70-405 and he felt a satisfyingly strong nudge against his shoulder. A fraction of a moment later, the buccaneer shrieked horribly as part of his throat tore away and a shower of blood rose in the air around him. Through the thinning wisps of smoke, Gaston saw his wife leap to her feet and sprint away from the defilement going on in the plaza.

A second after that, five carbines blazed in the direction of the low wall behind which Gaston Obraras sheltered. Three of the conical bullets penetrated and ripped apart his chest.

Gaston Obraras fell backward against the front of a cantina. His fading consciousness told him he had done his duty toward the woman he loved and that mattered even more. He sighed heavily and died.

With a smile on his lips.

Chapter 2

Majestically, like an oversized scarlet melon, the sun slid below the distant rim of the prairie. A tranquil afterglow bathed the prospering Dakota Territory town of Eagle Pass in its benevolent rays for an hour and a half beyond the time when the last thin slice winked out behind a far-off hill. During that interval, the "good" citizens of the frontier hamlet retired to their beds. Only the Thunder Saloon, with its cote of soiled doves, band of bartenders and duet of musicians remained ablaze with light and laughter.

Removed from this splash of gaiety, on the opposite side of town, hay rustled crisply in the loft of a large barn. A muted trill of laughter sounded in demure counterpoint to the tinkling of piano and ring of banjo in the community's only emporium of spirits. A man's bass voice rumbled in response to the feminine mirth.

"Hettie, this is all so—undignified."

She placed a small, soft palm on the front of his buckskin shirt. "Oh, Eli, what does that matter? It's also so different and—exciting."

Eli Holten, Chief Scout for the Twelfth U.S. Cavalry could not suppress his amusement or his ardor longer. A deep rumble sounded in his broad, powerful chest and he exposed even, white teeth in a smile of fondness.

"I give up, Hettie. You seem to have an unflagging knack for contriving the unusual."

"You like it, though, don't you?" the vibrant young woman purred.

Moonlight, through the open loft door, put silver highlights in her rich, dark brown hair. Snapping black eyes sparkled in the lambient rays and she tossed her small, well-shaped head in a provocative manner as she worked to undo the lacings of her Bavarian peasant-type blouse.

"It . . . uh, excites me in a way different from anything else," Eli admitted as he tugged at the hem of his leather shirt and pulled it upward. Suddenly, he felt himself caught up in some undefinable urgency.

"You're good for me, Hettie Dillon. Damned good," he added gruffly.

Hettie rose on tip-toe and thrust her pixie face close to his strong, square-jawed visage. Her full, sensuous lips parted slightly and she kissed him hard and breathlessly.

Eli Holten had known Hettie Dillon for over a year. She had been a passenger on a wagon train commanded by Yellowstone Frank Reamer. An incompetent, venal and vicious trail guide, Reamer had endangered the lives of those in his charge by attempting to evade an army dictum not to travel further westward during a strange dream-wandering migration by the Sioux, Cheyenne, Pawnee, and other plains tribes. He had further endangered their safety by firing on a peaceful band of Oglala. Only Eli's swift and powerful intervention prevented a massacre.

Later, even before Eli had led the immigrants to safety

in Eagle Pass, she and the scout had become lovers. Hettie had plans to teach at a superlative new school in Seattle. Her passion for Eli Holten, and a chance meeting with the Reverend Ezekial Smith changed all that. Now she primly pursued a career as schoolmarm in the one-room temple of learning built by the evangelist minister and presented to the town as a gift of love. Evenings, when Eli could make it to town from Fort Rawlins, she followed a less straight-laced track in the strong embrace of the scout. Since accepting the position, she had never been happier. Particularly when in the arms of Eli Holten.

Tongues mingled, flirted and parted, lips nibbled teasingly as their kiss ended. Gasping a bit in alarm at his ardor, Hettie touched his cheek lightly.

"My, we're eager tonight," she cooed sweetly.

"And you're not?" the scout inquired.

"Oh, Lordie, am I! Somehow . . . the days aren't the same when you're not here."

"It'll always be like that. I have my work . . ."

"You could quit," Hettie urged eagerly. "You could come and live here and I could continue teaching school."

"And be a kept man? No, Hettie, that sort of thing would never work."

"I *love you,* you lout! Don't you understand that? I don't care what you are, or what you do, or even if you do anything at all. I just want you near me."

Hettie Dillon had been the most demanding and facile love in Eli Holten's long experience. Their compatibility, and capacity for love-making, had been tested and tempered over the span of twelve months. Nothing was in doubt. Yet . . . this possessive streak often triggered warnings in the scout's mind. Some primordial instinct made him wary.

He shied at the sight of rice and white lace, cringed at the sound of wedding bells. The life of a civilian contract scout, at best, could be described as hazardous. At its worst, as during an Indian uprising, it could be downright fatal. He saw no rosy future for any woman tied to him. There would be no pension, not even extra compensation if the next day, or the next hour, he should have his skull shattered by a war club or his chest festooned with Sioux arrows. The crinkling of Hettie's starched dirndl blotted out that avenue of introspection.

Bare to the waist, Hettie's pert, young breasts stood out in stark relief against her slim build. Tiny rosebuds swelled and grew rigid as she leaned against the thatch of blond hair on Eli's chest and rubbed the sensitive nubs of flesh in a way that delighted them both. Her one hand went to his waist and probed behind the wide, thick belt that held his buckskin trousers in place.

Obligingly, Eli sucked in his muscle-ridged belly and allowed her egress. Her fingers, warm, soft and moist, searched eagerly among the coarse curls of his pubic thatch until they found and encircled the thick base of his long, achingly rigid phallus. He moaned softly in pleasure and Hettie echoed him.

Slowly she worked her way up the long, curved expanse of his tinglingly sensitive organ, squeezing and stroking as she went. Eli undid his belt and let his trousers drop. Freed now, his mighty shaft sprang outward under Hettie's guidance. With her short stature, it proved long enough to reach the flared arch of her rib cage. She rubbed his broad, dark red tip over the silken flesh of her taut belly and slid it downward.

Only her petticoats stood in the way, obstacles that Eli quickly removed. Nature cooperated with a shaft of silver that lighted her creamy complexion and emphasized each delightful curve and indentation. Passion's dew sparkled on the lush brown tufts that forested her swollen, moonlit mound. Her dark eyes sparkled with merriment and hunger. One hand at the small of Eli's back, the other directing his throbbing lance, she brought their most sensitive parts into exquisitely rapturous contact.

"Lie down," Hettie instructed. "Hurry, dearest. Aaah. That's it."

Eli raised his legs to provide her a back-rest as Hettie straddled his waist and lowered her open, inviting purse over the torrid arrowhead tip of his pulsating maleness. Eli shivered in joy as they made contact.

Ever so leisurely, Hettie consumed his manhood, easing bit-by-bit into the furnace cavern of her central core, made slippery with desire, heart pounding in counterpoint to the throbbing of her loins. Eli shuddered and arched slightly, thrilling to the elastic fluctuations that transmitted unbearable bliss through his raging organ to jangle every slightest nerve ending in his muscular, sun-browned body.

Tantalized by the novelty of their trysting place, Eli Holten knew that his night would be one to remember. At least, Eli thought gratefully, it would be an undisturbed one. There was no war going on at the time, he rejoiced, as ethereal abandon overpowered his reason and sent him off into a private world made only for lovers.

Low, golden streamers, given insensate life by rising dust motes, slanted in through cracks in the barn wall and ceiling. One aureate beam struck a floating nimbus of Hettie's topaz hair and turned it into a halo. Drowsily, Eli Holten watched it irridesce and followed the swirling macules that danced through the loft. He ran thick, work-roughened fingers through his heavy shock of long, curly yellow hair and combed out a collection of straw.

He itched, Eli realized in the next instant. His head, back and belly tingled with an accumulation of fine dust and sharp-edged specks of straw. He came upright in a lythe, cat-like motion and stared down on the delightful vision of Hettie Dillon, curled into a child's position of security, her radiant body glowing with health and the suffusing effect of lots of long and strenuous loving. She stirred slightly and he spoke.

"We have to be up and around, Hettie. It's daybreak already. And . . ." Eli paused while he scratched, "we both need a good soak to get rid of all this straw chaff and dirt."

Hettie dug at the few shallow folds in her peach-hued skin and tenderly touched the juncture of her thighs. She winced at the results.

"Me and my bright ideas," she acknowledged her own growing discomfort.

An hour later, refreshed and their coating of haymow scrubbed away, Eli and Hettie went for breakfast to the Ham 'n Grits, latest of a changing string of cafes that had opened and closed one after the other in Eagle Pass.

"What'll ya have, Eli, Hettie?" Mildred Sonners inquired when they took a small table near the back of the dining room.

"Coffee, Milly," Eli announced. "That before anything else. Then I want a double order of ham, grits, half a dozen eggs and some biscuits."

Mildred took Hettie's order and went away, to return with two steaming cups. Eli and the schoolmarm of Eagle Pass made light conversation while they waited for their meal to be served. From a table behind them, a man spoke loudly and drew Eli's attention.

"It's the army I'm tired of. I ain't tired of soldierin'. Too blamed many regulations gettin' in the way any more. Why, back in Sixty ta Sixty-five, a man didn't have much need of all them fancy written orders and all the inspections. It was shoot Rebs and raise general hell then."

"Face it, Sarge, it's war you like. You just can't abide all this peace."

The voice sounded rueful in reply. "Now, that's the truth of it. But I tell you, Corporal Dill, when your two day furlough is over, you go back to all those regulations and horse droppin's an' I'm goin' on to a nice little war."

"How's that?" the junior non-com inquired.

"I got me a letter from my brother. He's down in Mexico. Says the Mexicans need all the experienced soldiers they can get. That's why I didn't sign those re-enlistment papers this time."

"But, the *Mexican* army, Sarge?" Corporal Dill sounded scornful.

"Yep. Seems they have a regular little war goin' on in a place called Baja California." Sergeant Tyson pronounced the word "Baw-jaw."

"No wonder," Dill responded. "But . . . do you know the lingo?"

"Naw. Figger I can pick it up right fast enough. An' if they've got troubles in this Baw-jaw that only an old line so'jer like me can solve, I reckon they just might learn how to speak English rather fast."

Baja California. The name sent a shock of excitement through Eli Holten.

It had been a little more than a year since the abortive mutiny attempt at Fort Rawlins. A soldier named Howard Barryman and a man named Myron Henshaw had schemed to create the uprising to cover their plan to loot the fort of all the military equipment and arms they could haul away. Henshaw intended to take it to a freebooter named Madonna for an invasion of Baja California. At the time, Eli thought the idea preposterous. Now, it seemed, the attack had actually happened. Eli had another memory of that time, too. One not so pleasant to recall.

In addition to Barryman, Henshaw had another agent, working in secret. Constance Albright she had called herself. Later, Chief Scout Eli Holten had realized he had totally misread the signs. Connie had quite literally thrown herself at him. And he had caught the appealing package most willingly. Her mission had been to distract him, keep him away from the fort and Henshaw's design on the supplies. Constance Williams her name had actually been and, for three years, she had enjoyed the comforts and benefits of being Myron Henshaw's lover.

Eli felt foolish, sophomoric. Even now, as his skin tingled with growing warmth, he realized the memory could embarrass him. Hettie noticed and placed one small, warm hand on his arm.

"Is something wrong?"

"Uh . . . no. Nothing to worry you."

He had met Hettie during the mutiny and she became Connie's rival for his affections. Fortunately, as the scout saw it, Hettie remained ignorant of how he had been gulled. Led around by his pecker. What a galling thought.

"It's just something Tysōn said." Eli turned his spool-spindle straight-back chair and looked across the expanse of dingy, once-white tablecloth at the two soldiers. He caught the sergeant's eye and nodded.

"Sorry to hear you're giving up the army life, Grant," the scout began.

"'Ah, tis quite a life, without a wife, in the Regular Army-O,'" the non-com quoted the familiar song through a grin. "My time's up, Mister Holten. I thought I'd seek new horizons . . . some what don't have a Sioux lurkin' behind every bush and hill."

"What's this about Mexico?"

"My brother's down there, ranchin' cattle. Raises 'em there, drives north to market. He tells me there's some sort of invasion goin' on out California way. The Mexican part," he enlarged. "Some feller who styles himself as 'Iron Mike' Madonna has put together an army of desperados and such-like and attacked some place called Cabo San Lucas in the Baw-jaw."

"What more do you know about this little, ah, war?" Eli leaned forward, intent on any news Tyson might give him.

"Not a whole lot. Nobody does. Only that my brother wrote me that the Mexican commandante in Chihuahua is offerin' land grants for service by experienced soldiers who will go fight this Madonna feller. Approved by Mexico City an' all. Think of it. Me, a high-dalgo an' all. Pat-ron the Mexicans would call me after my time is up."

Milly brought the food and Eli turned back with a casual comment. "Good luck to you, Grant."

"Thank you, Mister Holten."

Through the meal, Eli seemed lost in speculation. He said little and ate mechanically. After he had paid and he and Hettie were once more on the street, she invaded his silence.

"You're planning something, I can tell."

"Humm? Uh, well, yes. You remember the mutiny last year? It was going on when we brought your wagon train here to Eagle Pass."

"Who could forget?" Hettie's warm, rich contralto held a hint of humor.

"The people responsible for it had planned to strip the fort of equipment and weapons and provide them to this Iron Mike Madonna for his little adventure. After what Tyson said, I think I'm going to look into it a little more."

"You're going to leave me. I know it."

"No." His reply came too quickly. "Uh, at least if I do, it will be for only a little while. Maybe I can give the Mexican government some ideas about their invader. Through channels, of course."

"Oh, of course."

Chapter 3

Juan Rubio fled with his whole family. Six children and Rosita, his dear and devoted wife. *Madre de Dios!* From where had these terrible *gringos* come? Juan's huarachis pattered a leather tattoo on the irregular surface of the narrow trail called a road. Ahead lay Todos Santos and, hopefully, sanctuary. Their youngest wailed and dug a grubby fist into one eye.

"*Calmate,* Hector," Juan scolded. "Only a little further, *niño.*"

Juan sincerely prayed that there was truth in what he said. Hoofbeats thundered from behind. Eyes round with apprehension, Juan looked over his shoulder as he continued to hurry along the track. He saw a blur of shiny motion. The next instant, eternity exploded behind his eyes.

Hector and the other Rubio children shrieked in uncontrollable horror as the sabre cut through their father's neck and his head leaped from his shoulders. The sharp report of a Springfield carbine silenced little Hector as his back erupted in a shower of blood. Ahead and to both sides, refugees fleeing the onslaught of Iron Mike Madonna's freebooter army died horribly, ridden down and slaughtered mercilessly by the ill-disciplined invaders.

"Save the women," one *gringo* called gleefully. "I'm hot to trot."

"Me, too," another English voice urged.

Rosita and several of the women made no attempt to fight the inevitable. Raised in a land of bandits and pillage, most had at least once been subjected to rape. Still in a state of shock over the brutal murder of her husband, she said nothing and made no move to resist when the three burly *gringos* came for her. They roughly stripped the clothing away from her. Pepe, her oldest son, leaped at the villainous soldiers, wielding a heavy field hoe.

One *gringo* laughed as he dodged the ten-year-old's swing and drew his revolver. Rosita moaned and turned away at the sound of the report. Hair and scalp erupted from the back of Pepe's head and he jerked backward, spasms wracking his body before he hit in the dust of the road. Although the sun shone brightly, Rosita shivered and tried to cover her nakedness.

Two of the murderers held her, while the third lowered his trousers, revealing a red and swollen member that poked impudently toward her. Her captors threw Rosita to the ground and she tried to make time stop. Hard hands clamped painfully on her ankles and pulled her legs apart. The one with the big *cholo* began to stroke it. *Punjeta,* Rosita thought scornfully. That was for little boys. Her tormentor dropped to his knees between her open legs and lowered himself into position.

Agony lanced through Rosita's dry and unwilling passage. Fiery shoots of misery jangled her nervous system. Her attacker grunted and snorted like a pig, his pale, white buttocks pumping up and down as he drove his hardened maleness into her. He seemed oblivious of her lack of lubrication. Then, as he thrust onward, she found, to her horror, that she had begun to respond.

Her heart beat faster and she felt all swimmy inside. Moisture poured into her savaged canal and she began to thrash her head from side to side. Panting, she bit at her lip to suppress groans of freshly kindled passion. It hurt.

No, it felt marvelous.

Her mind remained addled with horror over the brutal murder of her husband and two of her children, now she found her faithless body stimulated into eager, willing cooperation with the act being forced upon her.

Oh . . . oh how . . . good! The traitorous part of her body hummed with intense stimulation and she began to undulate her hips, matching the crude rhythm of the man who impaled her.

"Hey, Ike, Sam, she likes it. Can't get enough, huh, honey?" the rapist grunted as he continued to thrust. "Six kids, I guess so. Well, hang on, you got two more to go and then me again."

Rosita's juices flowed freely now. She made small, mewing sounds of delight as she tightened the muscles that controlled the elastic walls of her pleasure place. There would be more! Oh, oh, oh how it tingled and sang along her nerves.

"*Mas!*" she moaned. "*Mas. Tieso, tieso!*"

"That means, 'More. Harder, harder,'" Ike translated.

"Well, goll-damn. I think she likes me, boys."

"Hurry up," Sam complained. "My pecker's so stiff it's gonna pop open."

"Lope yer mule, Sam," Ike suggested. "I'm second."

"No you ain't." Sam looked around, determined to

find the release he so badly needed. His gaze settled on the frightened face of Teresa Rubio.

"There are four hundred eighty people in there," Iron Mike told Myron Henshaw. "Along with a platoon of Regulars and two light field pieces. They can cause us a world of hurt."

"Five hundred men stopped by forty greasers and a couple of six pounders?" Henshaw taunted. "Don't tell me."

"Watch your tongue, Henshaw, or I'll yank it out and feed it to Hannibal." Iron Mike nodded toward the broad-chested, sleek-headed mastiff that stood obediently at the side of his mount, steel spike collar gleaming brightly in the mid-morning sun. "The point you seem to fail to understand is that we are not obtaining any new recruits. So far all we've encountered are townspeople and peons. Until we can contact some of these hill bandits, and get them to join us, we need to conserve our forces. Every man lost is to be considered irreplaceable. It's a price we can't afford to pay. By evening the heavy guns will be brought up. Then we can sit out of range of those popguns of theirs and make them pay dearly. Hopefully they won't get it in mind to make a heroic charge against us in the meantime."

"What do you have in mind?" Henshaw asked, his dark, nearly colorless eyes glittering from the sun-browned smoothness of his face.

"We're going to put Todos Santos under siege."

"Oh, how jolly," a feminine voice injected with a note of sarcasm.

Iron Mike glowered. Taking a woman, any woman, into war was hardly his idea of an intelligent decision. To bring one like Constance Williams along seemed to him to be the height of madness.

She belonged in a fancy boudoir, wrapped in silks and furs, covered with jewels. A shiftless opportunist like Myron Henshaw didn't deserve a lady of quality like Constance. Her sea-green eyes and auburn hair heated his blood. Her voice, when she spoke softly, sweetly, could give him an erection that ached until he found some sort of release. Her body . . . God, he didn't dare think of what she must look like with that dusty brown riding habit removed, lying all pink and inviting on a bed. Those big, hard tits pointed at him like a pair of Gatling guns. She tormented him for being herself and, at the same time, reminded him of the woman he nearly married.

Milo Madonna had not always been a freelance soldier, working for whatever country or man of wealth needed his talents.

Young and idealistic, he had eagerly joined a volunteer regiment in his native Pennsylvania not long after the Rebels had fired on Fort Sumter. He rose quickly through the ranks and had received a battlefield promotion to second lieutenant prior to the regiment being sworn into the Union Army.

Despite the prejudice of the West Point men, he continued to advance in grade, at last being brevetted to full colonel. With courage, audacity and tactical brilliance, he won the respect of his superiors. He revolutionized the techique of the bayonette charge and, had his idea been given general acceptance, might have shortened the war by many months.

By use of small caliber, highly mobile artillery pieces, firing on the Confederate flanks, he had managed to keep the enemy attention on something of considerable importance while his infantry maneuvered by covert means into position for a short—usually not more than thirty yards—assault. Aided by enfiladed fire, his charging soldiers closed with the Rebels before the deadly artillery batteries of the Army of Northern Virginia could come to bear on his exposed men. There was little of the beloved dash and glory in it, but it worked. It gained for him the appellation of "Iron Mike." At the height of his career, he met and fell in love with a beautiful young woman.

Marie Chalmers represented everything the impressionable, twenty-three-year-old colonel ever dreamed of. Son of a hardworking, honest and talented cabinetmaker, Milo Madonna could only aspire to wealth and charm. Marie Chalmers had all that and more. Better still, she professed an undying love for Milo. He basked in a rosy glow of delightful enchantment. He asked her to marry him. She agreed. Nothing would ever be so perfect again, he profoundly believed.

Not until she managed to gain possession of some highly secret documents, pertaining to an imminent campaign that would wipe Robert E. Lee and his gray-clad army from the face of the earth, did he discover the terrible truth. After Marie had managed to spirit the maps and operations orders away to her superiors, Milo learned that Marie was a Confederate spy.

Crushed, embittered, he turned away from every form of sympathy or advice. He began to drink heavily, to be harsh toward his troops and brutally vindictive against Southern civilians who came under the jurisdiction of the advancing Union forces. His excesses reached the attention of the commander of the Army of the Potomac.

Ulysses S. Grant personally reduced Milo Madonna in rank to second lieutenant. Listless, uncaring, Milo drifted along. By the closing months of eighteen sixty-four, he had seen all of the Grand Army of the Republic he wanted to. Milo Madonna left the war three months before the final shot was fired.

He drifted into Mexico and, from there, to the small,

quasi-countries of Central America. He fought for any cause, hired out to any employer with enough money. Through the years, he attracted to his freebooter's banner other men of his type. Bitter, cynical, tough soldiers of a dozen nations came to fight under the leadership of "Captain" Madonna. His life's project, to carve out a nation for himself, came to him piecemeal. Once full-born, though, he wasted little time implementing his design. Quietly the call went out. Men came from Africa, Europe and all over the Latin States. Others, who found peace unappetizing after the years of conflict between the states, joined too. The riff-raff and criminal element came, also.

Iron Mike met Reynard Ballengier that way. Ballengier styled himself another Jean Lafite. What the French-Canadian pirate lacked in brilliance and firepower, he made up for in ruthlessness. Together they formed the final plan. With arms they obtained along the West Coast of Central America, and a sizable contribution of weapons which Henshaw eventually provided after a bloody raid on a small American arsenal, the army of adventurers invaded Baja California. Henshaw's initial failure in Dakota Territory still wrankled. That Henshaw brought along a woman for his own comfort salted Milo's wounded ego even more.

"We have enough men to see that no one enters or leaves Todos Santos," Iron Mike said abruptly. "Within two days, that will include by sea. Ballengier will be here with his ships. Then we make them sweat."

"But a siege," Henshaw countered. "Won't it seriously upset our schedule?"

"It might. Sieges are like opening an oyster," Iron

Mike philosophized. "You can go at it the hard way or spring the shells apart easily, with the right leverage. I intend to shuck the juicy heart out of Todos Santos with ease."

"No," General Frank Corrington exclaimed heatedly. "I can't spare you, Eli."

"Come on, Frank. There's nothing at all happening around here."

"Nothing? You call George Custer getting his command smeared all over the grass at the Little Big Horn *nothing?* The whole Department is in an uproar."

"Yes. But not here. The Sioux have run with Sitting Bull, or they're on their way back to the agencies. We are only operating five patrols out of Fort Rawlins. None from the Twelfth."

"That could change tomorrow," the general grumbled.

"Frank, you know why I want to do this. It's . . . damnit, it's a personal thing."

"Why? It was *my* command that had a mutiny. It was *me* the mutineers put in the guard house. *I* had to face the board of inquiry, not you. If anyone should want that son of a bitch, Myron Henshaw, it is me. Now, what's biting your ass, Eli?"

The general's angry rebuttal had cooled the scout's anger somewhat. "I . . . well, it's . . . it's Connie. She made a fool out of me. She and Henshaw planned that whole thing and left us both looking like idiots. I don't like being led around by the pecker."

Corrington snorted. "She did that, all right. But that didn't get in your way of breaking up the mutiny."

"That's not the point. I want to finish it with those two. I don't give a damn about this Madonna. The world survived Caesar and Napoleon, it can keep on turning with or without the good Captain. It's Henshaw I want. Henshaw and Constance Williams."

"So you're willing to run off to a foreign country, mix into a war that's none of your damned business and risk your life for the luxury of kicking a little ass? Foolishness!"

"It's not foolish if the insult hurts enough," Eli responded coldly.

Tenseness crackled in the atmosphere of the general's office. Frank Corrington and Eli Holten had been close friends for many years. Eli's second assignment with the army, as a civilian contract scout, had been to Frank's former command. When Corrington got his star and command of the cavalry squadron at Fort Rawlins, Holten went with him. Sinkingly, Eli could sense that this disagreement over the matter of Henshaw and Connie put a serious strain on their friendship. Helplessly, he realized he could do it no other way.

General Corrington rose from behind his desk and walked to the dark, rosewood sideboard. He rummaged among the bottles and came up with a dusty one filled two-thirds full of a dark, amber liquid.

"Jamaican rum. The best," he told his friend. "I'll pour you a glass, Eli. I knew about this invasion. Learned of it shortly after the attack on Cabo San Lucas."

"Why didn't you tell me?"

"What? And disturb your delightful evenings in Eagle Pass?" Corrington finished topping off the glasses and handed one piece of cut crystal to Holten. "In spite of your embarrassment over, ah, Connie, you seem to have done rather well for yourself."

"You can be a regular bastard at times, Frank," the scout offered through a grin.

"That's how you get your star, my boy. There may be bastards who aren't generals, but there's no general who isn't a bastard. Some of them, like Sherman and Custer made it a full-time occupation. Now, then, Iron Mike Madonna and his force, numbering some five hundred highly competent soldiers and another eighty auxilliaries, are moving up the peninsula of Baja California. They have, at the last report, taken several towns, sacked them and moved on. Their eventual goal is believed to be the bay and the excellent port facilities at La Paz. Ironically, the name means, 'The Peace.' There's gold, silver and lead mines in the path of this mob of locust.

"Anything seems to be fair game. They specialize in looting, rape and murder. To the best of my knowledge, Myron Henshaw and Constance Williams are not with this horde of invaders. Although, it is believed that the small arsenal at Rock Creek, Arizona Territory, was broken into and the contents stolen by a gang led by a man whose description is quite similar to Henshaw."

"I'm willing to bet my job Henshaw did it. And that they are with Madonna."

The general looked grim. "That's exactly what you will be doing. If you go mucking around in another country's internal problems, you can get your tit in a wringer faster than a new whore loses her cherry."

"'What *I* will be doing?' That sounds like you're going to give me the time I asked for."

"I shouldn't. I'm as big an idiot as you are for doing so, Eli. But . . . damn it, they made a fool of me, too. Go get those two and do whatever in hell you want to them.

Ah . . . provided you don't let that woman get you in bed again. You'd never be the same. Now, get out of here."

"Yes, General. Anything you say, sir."

"Don't be a smart-ass, Eli."

Holten pulled a long face. "And to think . . . this time I don't even get a cigar."

Chapter 4

Three days!

Now, on the morning of the fourth, Diego Rivera could hardly believe that Todos Santos had held out that long. By the Grace of God, he added hastily.

He finished shoving the last of the .44-40 cartridges into the loading gate of the modern, smoothly-operating Winchester rifle. A gift, if one could call it that, he thought warmly. Little Joselito Moreno had risked his life to retrieve it and a box of one hundred rounds from one of the fallen invaders.

There had been a sortie against one side of town. A diversion, caused by artillery fire on the low wall and arched gateway on the main road, had taken the attention of the defenders while a small force approached along a route between the bay and the outskirts of town. It would have worked if Lupe Bargas hadn't observed the stealthy approach and given the alarm.

Five of the *gringos* had died in that assault. None of the precious few townsmen. *Voluntad del Dios.* Was it also the will of God that he become a fighter, a leader of the resistance to this invasion? Diego Rivera rose at the sound of approaching footsteps and adjusted his cassock.

"*Padre* Diego," Alberto Montez, the *alcalde*, greeted him. "There is grave news. Two ships are standing off the mouth of the bay. I'm afraid they are with the men who attack us."

The priest turned and stalked to a window, deep-set in the thick adobe wall of the rectory. Ornately worked wrought-iron grillwork barred it and Father Diego looked through the vertical strips toward the sea. A frown creased his smooth brow.

Yes. He saw them.

Although he could not make out detail, the dark rectangle flying at the masthead of each vessel must be the jolly roger. Pirates in this day and age? Walking the plank, buried treasure? Father Diego nodded sparingly. It fitted the madness of this whole misadventure.

"Mister Mayor, Alberto my son," the priest said, sighing heavily. "We are doomed. With ships' guns to the west of us and artillery on the other three sides, all they need do is reduce Todos Santos to heaps of rubble. Perhaps the lives of the innocent would be spared if we were to surrender to this Captain Madonna."

Gray-haired Alberto Montez looked at the padre. Diego calls a man twice his age "my son." The Church taught him that, the mayor thought resignedly. It also taught him to turn the other cheek, to pursue the ways of peace and love. But he is also a fighter, this Diego Rivera.

"*Mierda!*" Montez exploded. "How can a man bear the name of the Mother of God and be such a demon? The refugees who came to us ahead of *Capitán* Madonna and his *monstruosos* tell of pillage and rape, of the defilement of children. I saw with my own eyes what was done to that little girl not a hundred paces from the city gate."

While the mayor spoke, *Padre* Diego had been

watching a small boat put out from behind the lines of the besiegers. It headed for the ships, which drew nearer on the slight morning breeze. One man stood erect amidships.

"I saw it too," the priest spat in frustration. *"Perdona me Dios, por que estar para hacer."*

Diego Rivera raised the Winchester to his shoulder and sighted on the man standing in the boat. *Forgive me Lord, indeed,* he thought, *for what I am about to do.*

Behind his conscious act, a repulsive vision danced, of a small girl, her lips closed around the reddened obscenity of a *gringo* soldier's penis. Father Diego raised his sights slightly and his finger tightened on the trigger. A difficult shot for any man.

The Winchester cracked and blossomed smoke. A long moment passed, then the upright passenger lurched to the side, reeled drunkenly and fell into the bay.

"Gracias a Dios," the priest exhaled. He turned to the mayor. *"Señor Alcalde,* is it blasphemy to thank God for helping you kill?"

Reassured now, Alberto Montez smiled. "I don't know, *Padre.* It is you who are the priest. We have much to do."

"Many innocent will die in a concentrated shelling."

"I know. Do we call it our burden? Our cross to bear? Tell me, *Padre,* where did you learn so much of military affairs? You're hardly over thirty. Yet, you anticipate nearly every move these *mercenarios* make."

Father Diego produced a sheepish grin. "For my sins, I read books on the great battles of history. I admire the famous generals. Their plans and strategies are much like a gigantic chess game."

Montez smiled, remembering how easily and how often

he had beaten the cleric at chess. "You don't shoot like a chess player, or a reader of books."

"A hobby. I like to hunt quail and other small game."

"A contradiction, *Padre?* I don't imagine you do so on *El Dia de San Francisco.*"

"Hardly." Diego produced a tight grin. "Though I must confess I have often debated if that would constitute a mortal sin were I to do so. Now, we need an updated inventory of the food, water and ammunition available. Also, the small cannon must be put under our direction. *Teniente* Ordoñez does not understand the proper employment of artillery. Why should he? He is a *lancero.* The two pieces must be kept in their limbers so that they may be moved rapidly from place to place."

"Did you see that shot?" Myron Henshaw exclaimed. "I would never have believed it."

"Are you cheering for the enemy now, Myron?" Connie Williams asked cooly.

"Of course not. Only . . . these greasers aren't such outstanding marksmen. I wonder who did it?"

"The shot came from the rectory," Connie told him.

"You . . . mean . . . a *priest?*" Somehow, the idea disturbed the hardened outlaw.

"Who else lives in the rectory of a church?"

"I don't give a damn if it was the Pope himself," Iron Mike Madonna snapped. "Whoever did it killed the only officer, besides myself, who speaks French. We'll have a hell of a time coordinating the final assault with Ballengier."

"You could always write his orders out," Henshaw suggested.

"If I could read and write in French," Iron Mike growled.

A light on-shore breeze stirred the tight curls of Captain Madonna's dusty-blond hair. He scratched absently at an ear lobe as he studied the small city that still defied him. Three days they had managed to hold out. Now, as the morning of the fourth wore on, he began to wonder if Henshaw hadn't been right about the disruption of their timetable. Would the Mexican government move fast enough to send sufficient troops from the mainland? What if this delay got them to La Paz only to face a full division of Mexican infantry and all the usual artillery and light cavalry support?

"I speak enough French to make things clear to Captain Ballengier," Connie injected with a deprecating smile.

"A *woman* giving orders to a pirate captain! What in he . . . ?" Suddenly Iron Mike began to laugh. "You know, I like that. Ballengier will bust a blood vessel when he sees who I send him to be my liaison officer. All right, Miss Constance, we'll do it that way."

Briskly Iron Mike strode to a low field table where he had laid out a sketch of Todos Santos and the area around the bay. He pointed a thick finger at the estuary, the *melecón* and the row of shops and warehouses beyond. Slowly he traced a line through them.

"Here's where Ballengier's gunners are to aim their first broadsides. Exactly six, no more or less. Then he's to raise the guns and fire on the center of town. Blast that damned church into rubble. Tell him that under no circumstances is he to get any stray shots to the north or south of the areas I've shown you. No long rounds, either. My men will be attacking while he continues to shell. Just like Santiago."

"And . . . if Captain Ballengier refuses to take advice from a woman?" Connie inquired.

Iron Mike looked up and down and produced a lascivious grin. "You can . . . ah, convince him."

"What are you getting at, Madonna?" Henshaw asked querulously.

"*Captain* Madonna, if you don't mind. I was merely pointing out that even if Ballengier is a pirate and a superstitious seaman, he is also French. In light of that, I think you should agree that Miss Constance is excellently equipped to handle any of his objections."

"Unnh!" Henshaw grunted, not the least mollified.

"We will attack at noon, when most everyone in town is home eating."

At first the steady rumble of thunder pleased him. They needed rain in the parched desert around Todos Santos. Father Diego Rivera had been napping after a light lunch of *caldo de cammarón,* tortillas and some cheese. When he came fully awake, he realized that the dull booming came from cannon. The *gringo* mercenaries had begun another attack.

"Get word to everyone to man their stations," *Padre* Diego told a small boy standing in the doorway to his bedroom. "Hurry, Pablo."

"*Sí, Padre. Inmediatamente.*"

Father Diego gathered his rifle and the rust-spotted old revolver before he headed out to get an overall view of the assault that would surely come soon. In the street, people ran in confusion, eyes wide and white with fear.

Over the rooftops, from the hill where the church sat, he saw the billows of smoke wreath the tall sides of the two ships. A moment later the flat reports of the guns reached his ears. Roundshot howled through the air like angry giant bees.

Dirt and oyster shells leaped in the air from the *melacón*. In the distance, nearer where the cannonballs fell, a child shrieked in pain. From behind and one side, more artillery spoke and houses at the edge of Todos Santos shuddered from impact. Great chunks of plastered adobe broke from them and fell in a dusty cascade. Where would the attack come from? *Padre* Diego pondered that as he hurried in search of the mayor.

"They are massing for a big attack," Alberto Montez informed the priest three minutes later.

"I gathered that," *Padre* Diego responded dryly. "The problem is, where?"

"I would say to the south of the city."

"Why is that, Alberto?"

"There is no cannon fire there."

The priest favored him with a smile of approval. "You're learning, Alberto. We'll make a soldier of you yet."

"I'm a politician. Mayor of Todos Santos. I have no need to be a soldier."

"We all do in these days, Alberto. Send the good *Teniente* Ordoñez and his cannon to the south wall, then."

"He thinks they will go for the gate over the main road."

"They are not lancers as he is," Diego chided mildly. "Have him do as he is directed."

"*Sí, Padre.* It shall be as you wish."

In-coming artillery drowned out further conversation as the freebooters intensified their barrage prior to launching waves of troops at the beleaguered city. Earth and stone erupted, to fall noisily among the screams of the injured and dying. Tears came to Father Diego's eyes and he doubted again his decision to continue to resist. A shout rose as *gringo* soldiers appeared beyond the wall to the south, running, bent low, toward the town. Scattered musketry crackled in defiance. Then came the sharp bark of Lieutenant Ordoñez's six pounders.

"*Ay, hijo de la chingada!*" a uniformed corporal in the lieutenant's squad cursed a dozen yards from Father Diego. "There are more coming from the north."

A maimed child ran screaming across the plaza, blood streaming in a crimson sheet from the ragged stump of his severed arm. He made it to the central fountain before he collapsed and lay in a quivering heap. Sickness surged in Father Diego's stomach. So many to die. So young and helpless.

"The ships!" old Humberto Cruz shouted. "They are shooting at the church, *Padre.*"

Fat chips of adobe flew from one corner of the stout-walled building. Hot bits of jagged shrapnel hummed menacingly through the air from exploding roundshot. Suddenly the *gringos,* who wore an odd assortment of clothing but fought like disciplined, well-trained troops, swarmed into the streets of Todos Santos.

Men screamed and died, fighting in small knots and clusters, defending their homes against the implacable invaders. Resistance weakened, faltered. Father Diego tried to be everywhere at once.

"The church! Hurry to the church," he shouted over and over. "We can hold them off there."

Some of the townspeople listened. The women and children first. They streamed toward the *plaza de armas* and the beckoning shelter of their church. A few of the men followed. Father Diego emptied his Winchester into a flying wedge of the besiegers, downing five of them, then he, too, hurried toward the big, oak doors.

"Inside," he urged. "Bar the doors."

Nearly invincible behind the thick walls and sturdy doors, with food and water supplies good for at least a week, the defenders of Todos Santos could have held out against their enemy. They would have, if the torturing hadn't begun.

Shrieks of agony came from women, children and old people who had been unlucky enough to be caught before entering the sanctuary. Some of the priest's male parishioners, who had fought bravely, had been spared by the invaders, only to be dragged into the plaza and forced to their knees, while the fiendish marauders tormented them with knives and hot irons. Father Diego Rivera's conscience would not bear the terrible burden. He ordered a white flag to be shown from the belfry.

Strutting insolently, the captors entered the church. The man in charge, obviously a natural leader, pointed out the priest and several others, including the mayor.

"I am Captain Madonna. You are all my prisoners. Those who did not fight against my men will be spared. As for the rest . . ." Iron Mike turned to the man on his left. "Take these men out against the wall. Organize a firing party."

Familiar enough with English, Father Diego realized

the import of what had been said. A firing party. They were to be executed. Martyred. So be it.

Head held high, chest out and shoulders square, the shepherd of the Todos Santos flock led the way out of his church and to the place indicated. He waited calmly while a motley collection of the hard-faced raiders assembled in a line before them. They resembled nothing so much as the scuffy hill-bandits who preyed on the unwary travelers and frequently swept down on smaller, unprotected villages. At a shouted order, the firing squad came to attention. Father Diego stepped forward.

"Wait!" he called in accented English. "Let me at least give these poor souls the last rites."

At a sign from the leader, the young officer commanding the firing squad ordered the men to lower their weapons.

"Go ahead, *Padre*," a rumbling baritone voice replied.

"*Gracias.* Thank you." Father Diego made a large sign of the cross over the kneeling men. "*Ego vos absolvo de pecatis vostrum in nomine Patris, et Filii et Spiritus Sancti. Amen,*" he declared in Latin. "Receive, oh God," he went on in Spanish, "the souls of these faithful departed."

When the prayers ended, Iron Mike Madonna gave a signal.

"De-tail . . . at-tention! . . . Ready! . . . Aim! . . . Fire!"

A ragged volley sounded and the victims of this unholy execution went rigid as the bullets struck. Blood sprayed the church wall behind them. They pitched into the dirt of the street as scarlet streams welled from ragged exit wounds. A few cried out in the moment of extremis, then all lay twitching out the last of their lives. A groan of anguish came from Father Diego's lips when he discovered that he had not been shot with the others.

"I want him for myself," Constance Williams announced as if in answer to the priest's unspoken question.

"No!" Iron Mike's shocked voice cracked.

"Oh, yes. I want to see him cringe, this black crow in his woman's dress. I want to watch his blood fly." A wild, fanatical light glowed in Connie's eyes and she licked her lips in a sick parody of lust.

"Idol-worshipers, eaters of human flesh, eunuchs, defilers of children . . ." the invective poured from Connie's mouth like offal from a sewer.

She stepped forward and, as she did, drew the Merwin and Hulbert revolver that rested in a high, back-raked holster at her hip. She eared back the hammer and, before Iron Mike or any of his men could act to stop her, shoved the muzzle into Father Diego Rivera's left ear.

"Die, you Papist carrion bird of Rome!" she screamed as she squeezed the trigger.

Muffled by the muzzle's contact with his skin, the report sounded flat and dull. The .44 bullet blasted apart brain tissue and blew away the opposite side of Father Diego's head. Before it did, hot gasses entered his skull and expanded, bulging the priest's eyes and pulping the cortical matter. Jolted to the side, Father Diego's body remained suspended for a moment at a wierd angle, his right ear hanging obscenely down against the neck, held by a strip of flesh.

Horror numbed Carmella Morales' mind as she

witnessed the awful scene of Father Diego's execution. She trembled and tears ran from her shiny black eyes. Hands to her mouth to prevent betraying cries of anguish, she looked on as the cleric's body tumbled into the dirt with the others. So far, she had been lucky.

She had hidden in the "priest's hole," a small secret compartment behind the high altar of the church. Designed in the twelfth century, during the wicked persecutions of the Faith by Prince John in England and other despots on the Continent, the hiding place had saved the life of more than one cleric. Burned into her memory was the hateful image of the woman who had butchered the beloved Father Diego. One day, Carmella promised herself and God, she would avenge this senseless, wanton murder. First, though, she had to escape from Todos Santos.

She had come from her hiding place at the sound of the volley which ended the lives of the last defenders of Todos Santos. Now she thought only of surviving. She would go first to her family in El Triunfo.

Her brothers would know what to do. How to stop these demons from Hell. They had guns and the blasting powder for use in their mine. The other men respected them and would follow the *Hermanos* Morales in an uprising. Yes. Get away and find her brothers. Then, she planned as she tip-toed silently back through the church, she would go on to La Paz and tell the governor of the horrors being visited upon their country. The *soldados* would come and soon these *gringo ladrónes* would dangle from trees all over the mountains of Baja Sur.

In the vestry, she cut away her long, black hair with the sharp kitchen knife she had brought with her to defend her honor if need be. Only a small whimper of regret accompanied the loss of her beautiful tresses. Then she dressed in the chasuble and alb of an altar boy. After a careful glance in all directions, she slipped out a side door and fled from the horror in the square.

Already her ears rang with the screams of the young women and girls being raped by the conquerors.

Chapter 5

Even at mid-morning, the odor of charcoal fires mingled with the effluvium of open sewers and human misery over the Mexican city of Hermosillo. Eli Holten had used a variety of means to arrive there. He had taken the steam packet from Pierre in Dakota Territory to Saint Joseph, Missouri, then a combination of trains and stage coaches to South Texas, where he crossed over into Mexico and once more rode the iron rails to Hermosillo. His journey to Mazatlan would be but an extension of this latter trip.

"*Atención! Viajeros a Guymas, Ciudad Obregón, Los Mochis, Culiacan y Mazatlán, a bordo tren numero diez y sies . . .*" A short, bulging-bellied man in a tan uniform cried through a megaphone.

Although he didn't understand the language, the scout recognized the name of the city he journeyed to. He picked up his saddle, bedroll and large carpetbag and started toward the gate where a shuffling line of men and women with dark, Indian faces and white cotton clothing formed to board the train. Once through the gate, two other men in khaki uniforms directed people to the proper cars. Each held a large sign with the number 16 on it. Eli looked at the printing on his ticket and twisted his mouth into shape to pronounce the bold-faced words.

"Primera Classa," he informed the *acomodador.*

"Ay, sí. A derecho. El ultimo carro," he directed Eli.

The last car. To his surprise, since arriving in Mexico, the price of transportation was so low that Eli could afford a stall in the livestock car for Sonny and first class accommodations for himself. He walked briskly in the indicated direction and found a porter anxiously waiting to help him with his belongings.

"Right in here, sir," the porter chattered on in Spanish as he bowed and showed Eli into a small compartment.

Not bad, the scout thought. An overhead bunk, a removable table, two padded bench seats facing each other front and rear. A rose-glass shade covered the chimney of a small kerosene lamp that hung from a brass bracket between the two windows. Red flocked wainscotting had been added below the stamped tin wall-covering and the ceiling of the same metal material showed the stains of long usage. Three days to Mazatlán, then by sailing ship to La Paz. At least his time could be pleasantly spent.

"Gracias," the scout responded with one of his few, newly acquired words of Spanish. He handed the porter a thick five peso coin. Then he got about the business of settling in.

Twenty minutes later, No. 16 pulled noisily out of the station. Black smoke, dust and cinders swirled about the cars as they lurched, squeaked and rattled clamorously. Eli soon got bored with the yellow, rust and gray sameness of the desert terrain. The dining car, he knew, would be ahead, near the center of the train. So would the bar car, *La Cantina del Ferroviario* as the information plaque on the inside of his door put it. He would go forward and have a couple of good, rich tasting Mexican beers before the noon meal.

Crowded with others of like mind, the bar car offered no convenient place for Eli to sit. At a small table by the left-hand windows, an expensively dressed, handsome gentleman with neatly trimmed mustache and long, thin sideburns sat alone. He smoked a cigar and sipped some form of clear liquid from a fluted glass. An empty chair beckoned from across the table.

"Excuse me," Eli began in a subdued voice. "Is that chair taken?"

"Ah! You speak English," the man responded. "No. Make yourself comfortable."

"Thank you. I'm Eli Holten." Eli offered his hand to be shaken.

"*Con mucho gusto, señor*. I am Major Carlos Antonio Maria Ocampo, at your service."

"You are in the army?"

"No. A *Federale*. The, ah, Mexican National Police. We are, though, strictly a para-military organization. We wear uniforms, have titles of rank and ride in formation—much like your, ah, Texas Rangers." Ocampo pronounced the name of the state in the Mexican manner—Tay-has.

"Well, then, we have something in common. I'm on leave, visiting Mexico for pleasure. I am a civilian contract scout for the U.S. Army."

Ocampo raised eyebrows. "A spy? Is there then to be another invasion of Mexico?"

Eli laughed. "Not that I know of. I'm here on my own."

"Then you are welcome, *Señor* Hol-ton," Ocampo answered, though he stumbled over the name.

"Let's make it easy. I'm Eli and you're Carlos."

"Good enough. Will you share with me a glass of tequila?"

"I'd thought to have a beer or two, but I have an open mind."

Ocampo beamed, showing large, even white teeth. "Fine idea. *Cantinero!*" he called out, snapping his fingers. "*Dos tequilas y una cerveza Bohemia.*"

Drinks were brought and the two men began to discuss similarities and peculiarities of their services. The conversation continued until lunch time. Eli waited a while before introducing the topic that most interested him.

"I understand that you have a bit of a small war going on in Baja California?"

Ocampo scowled and brushed a spatulate brown fingertip at his pencil-line mustache. "Unfortunately that is true. The peninsula is so . . . ah, isolated. An expeditionary force is being prepared of crack troops from *La Capital.* But—" Ocampo shrugged expansively and made a wobbling gesture with one hand, palm down. "Who knows how long it will take? Here in Mexico we have an expression: *Mañana tambien es un otra dia.* Tomorrow is also another day."

"But, if these invaders are allowed time to consolidate their positions, won't it be more difficult to dislodge them?"

"*De veras!* Exactly! I'm only a lowly policeman, but even I can see this. It's . . . risky. Foolhearty. Even so—" Ocampo sighed heavily. "Nothing moves quickly here, my friend."

"In a way, I feel responsible for this war."

"How's that?" A frown creased Ocampo's smooth, high forehead.

"There are two people, whom I suspect of being with the invading force. They attempted to steal munitions, weapons and supplies from Fort Rawlins, where I am assigned. Their scheme failed, but they escaped. Later, an arsenal in Arizona was raided and many weapons stolen. The odds are the theft was organized by Myron Henshaw. I let Henshaw get away at Fort Rawlins. Not intentionally, but—" Eli shrugged.

"You take it too personally. What will be will be. Enough of this talk. Do you play at cards?"

"A little."

"Marvelous. Perhaps you would care to join me and some gentlemen after *siesta* for a few hands?"

"It would be a pleasure, Carlos. Thank you."

Hot and sticky, the thick blood flowed in a torrent over Carmella Morales' hands and forearms. To her surprise, the *gringo cabrón* had not cried out. His only sound had been a surprised little gasp when the long, thin blade slid deep into his belly.

His eyes widened, tears formed, then his lust-distorted expression slackened and sagged and he swiftly went soft within her. Repulsed by his person, his repeated act and her swift killing, she exerted all her effort to shove him off her slippery body. Washed crimson by his saguinary outflow, she felt the sour broth of revulsion rising in her throat. *Por Dios!* Only another day and she would have gotten away safely.

Carmella had made good her escape from Todos Santos in the guise of an altar boy. All that long afternoon when the city fell to the invaders she had alternated walking and trotting along the road northward. She had paused at sundown long enough to pare and eat some ripened cactus fruit and some tortillas she had brought from home. Then she hurried on until fatigue felled her at last, some indeterminate time after midnight. Advance scouts of the *gringo* invasion caught up to her the next morning.

At first they had toyed with her, like *gatos* with a mouse. Then they grew serious, vicious and very direct. First, the fat one, who smelled of garlic and stale piss, grabbed her and ripped away her clothing. While his companion held her helplessly against the ground, he unfastened his trousers and let them fall. He revealed an almost tragically funny collection of fleshly miniatures.

His short, thick penis hardly penetrated her outer portals. Yet, he had raped her as thoroughly as if he had the equipment of a stallion. It had been the violation of her mind and her will that had so utterly disgusted her.

Shamed, feeling dirty, she had laid beside the trail, shivering, and huddled to hide her humiliation. Then this one, Brown he called himself, had taken his will on her.

From the beginning she had sensed a difference. Slowly, almost diffidently, he had turned her over on her back. Shyly, he had spread apart her blood-smeared thighs. Almost apologetically, he had pressed his entirely naked body against hers. Then, with the hesitancy of a small boy on his first occasion, he entered her.

To her unexpressible surprise and growing delight, his

every move became a gentle communication of something other than anger or contempt. Gradually, her cold, aching body began to warm to this treatment, to glow and respond. The walls of her passage grew moist and began to contract in time to his thrusts. She mewed and moaned.

She licked at his ear, then his face. Her breath grew ragged and hot, drawn in short gasps as she raised her legs to clinch him tightly. Her heart pounded and she cried out with wild abandon as she crashed over the peak and shuddered in delight. Carmella clawed at his back and left long, scarlet trails to remind him of the passion they shared. She thrashed her head from side to side and thrilled to another monstrous explosion that built as he went rigid and gushed forth a long, burning stream of his life force.

Then her Vesuvius erupted in a mind-shattering totality and wailing together, they disintegrated into oblivion. An eternity later, they had whispered of their enjoyment, each in a language unintelligible to the other. He said he wanted more of her and she gave, freely, eagerly. Enough, at least, that he had quickly come to trust her. He argued with his companion to take her along, and won. Another night and day went by. Then, safe in his confidence, she had managed to get back her knife.

Moments earlier, as they lay in the throes of passion, she had used it. With a shudder, Carmella brought herself back to reality. She had let her mind wander while she slid from under the dead weight of the *gringo*. A feral grin made a white slash in her slightly narrow, angular face as she eased her way over the ground to where the garlic-smelling invader snored brutishly, like a pig in rut. She paused briefly over his recumbent form. The knife flashed a moment in the moonlight and arched downward.

This time she made no effort to be quiet. A most satisfactory scream tore from the distorted lips of the *gringo* bandit as her blade plunged deeply into his stomach. Ruthlessly, she yanked the knife one way, then the next, across the rigid drum of his abdomen.

Flesh parted and the scream turned to a shriek of unbearable agony. Slowly, as she brought the edge upward to test the rigid dome of his diaphragm, the sound changed to a gurgling howl. Pink bubbles formed and popped on his lips. His eyes, wide, white and wild, pleaded with her.

"Next time you ask Carmella politely, eh?" Carmella told him in Spanish. "You remember that, *hijo de la puerca.*"

Swiftly, then, the light went from his eyes. He died with the trembles of a palsied old man. Carmella cleaned the knife and herself in the nearby basin of a seep-spring and dressed carefully in items chosen from loot in their saddlebags. She still had a long way to go to El Triunfo. At least now, she thought with a certain malicious satisfaction, she had a horse to ride there.

Major Ocampo had the bid. As his partner, Eli Holten sat back and enjoyed the hand. The *Federale* officer had proven an astute card player the previous evening. He and Eli had easily defeated the two gentlemen from Guadalajara two sets in a row for three games.

Determined to recoup, the amiable cardplayers had insisted on a rematch following the midday meal, next day. Carlos and Eli were only too glad to oblige.

Their contest had extended long into the *siesta* period. A heavyset, droopy-eyed waiter remained on duty in the bar car to tend their needs. Whist might well be an international game, but these citizens of Mexico played it as though national honor rested on the outcome, Eli observed to his amusement. The stakes, which had started off modestly enough, had now progressed to the point where they hazarded roughly the equivalent of fifty dollars U.S. per set, a dollar a point and the third set played in each game whether needed or not. With grim determination, the men from the far-off state of Jailisco went about assessing another defeat. Across from him, Eli noted that Carlos seemed equally entertained by the intensity of their opposition.

Carlos led a low trump. His opponents scowled. Eli had been right in his count. Between them they had all the useful counters in the trump suit. This final set of the game would be a disaster for their competition.

It proved to be worse than that.

Screeching loudly, the train wheels locked up and the solid wooden coaches lurched as forward movement rapidly slowed. Cards went flying, along with glasses and heavy metal stands. Over the tumult, Eli heard the clear, stacatto sound of gunfire.

"*Bandidos!*" the conductor shouted as he ran forward. He groped in a ceiling-high box at the end of the car and came out with a loaded revolver.

"Curse this luck," Major Ocampo spat as he reached under his jacket for his own weapon. "Bandits right when we had those two at our mercy."

Gunfire roared louder and the glass disintegrated in the window next to Eli Holten's head.

"Wonder if those fellers out there would enjoy a hand of Whist?" the scout asked calmly as he produced his sturdy Remington revolver and took aim on the unshaven face of a howling bandit riding by a few feet outside the broken window at his side.

Chapter 6

Scarlet mist surrounded the unfortunate bandit's head for an instant after Eli Holten shot him through his open, screaming mouth. A startled, disbelieving expression formed on the outlaw's face, as though he could not accept that one of those he had come to rob would fight back. Then he fell from his saddle, under the trampling hoofs of his companions' horses.

"One less," the scout observed to Major Ocampo.

Worry lines crinkled the corners of the *Federale's* eyes and wrinkled his brow. "There are only, ah . . . six soldiers on board. I count some fifteen *bandidos.*"

"On this side," Eli added.

"*Sí*. On this side," Ocampo lamented.

Heavy bullets smacked into the thick wooden sides of the railcars. Glass broke in more windows and women screamed in fright. Ahead, the steam whistle shrieked a frantic message for help, then went ominously silent.

"This happen often, Carlos?" Holten inquired as he maneuvered for a better shot at their assailants.

"All too frequently, *amigo,*" the federal cop answered through a tight, sardonic grin. "We are spread too thin and there are too many bandits. Hunger can make *ladrónes* of us all."

"What's the significance of the soldiers?"

Carlos grew rueful. "They are to, ah, protect us from *bandido* raids."

"Someone forgot to tell the bandits," Eli answered as he took aim on another of the thieves who had ridden in close.

Thick and meaty, the train robber absorbed two .44 rounds from Eli's Remington before he swayed drunkenly and dropped forward onto his mount's neck. An instant later, the door at the far end of the car behind Eli slammed open. A tall, lean man stood in the entrance, dressed all in brown, with a wide brimmed sombrero, high boots and a brace of revolvers. The thin black line of mustache that formed a half-circle around his small mouth writhed like a snake as he pumped alternating slugs from the blazing muzzles of his weapons.

A hot, painful line ripped across the back of Eli's shoulders as he pivoted in that direction. An eye-blink later, Holten triggered his six-gun.

A dark hole appeared right in the center of the bandit's crossed bandoliers of ammunition. Blood began to well from its depths as he backpeddled out onto the vestibule. He triggered one bullet into the ceiling and another into the floor. His eyes rolled upward in his head, and he sighed with resignation as he fell over the low iron rail that separated the carriages. Two more hill raiders took his place.

Carlos shot one through the throat and the man crumpled bonelessly to the floor, spraying a shower of blood. The other darted toward the door to the next car back.

"There are other coaches to rob," he declared

philosophically as he disappeared inside.

Eli began to reload the Remington. His ears strained to hear the heavy blast of military rifles. He heard none.

"Those soldiers aren't doing much protecting," the scout observed as he slid the last cartridge into his revolver.

Carlos sighed. "I fear they may have been killed first. Or those who survived are hiding, keeping safe."

"Which leaves only us."

"And a few others. We can wait no longer. We must attack the *bandidos.*"

Eli smarted from the bruise the near-miss had caused. "Say, I hate to mention it, but . . . this *is* your country and they *are* your bandits."

"You bleed and die just the same here as in *Los Estados Unidos,* do you not?"

"You have a point. I'll work my way forward, see what's happened."

"And I'll follow that *cabrón* who ran from us," Carlos offered.

Holten found the dining car a shambles of broken glass, dishes and frightened passengers. A frantic woman clutched imploringly at his ankle as he inched along through the litter. From ahead, a rapid spate of gunfire rattled and the scout heard at last the solid boom of a .45-70 rifle. Ignoring the frightened pleas of the diner's occupants, he made his way in that direction.

Bandits swarmed around the next car. Holten stepped in closer.

"Hey, you," he called out cheerfully.

"High juu?" a runty bandit with a mouthful of snaggled teeth asked as he started to turn, puzzled over the foreign sounds.

Eli Holten eliminated some of the overcrowding behind the robber's lips with a little .44 caliber oral surgery. Fragments of several overlapping canines and incisors went flying as a hot slug bulled its way into the outlaw's jaw and exploded bone and ivory in a rosy shower. A fraction of a second later, the scout cut down on another would-be bandit.

A perfect figure eight formed on the left side of the gunhawk's chest. His heart burst as two sizzling 225 grain bullets ripped through and erupted out his back. The third *bandido* threw a knife.

Eli jerked his head a bit to the left as the cold steel swished past his ear and thudded into the wood of the car. An unbidden smile twisted the scout's lips as he eared back the hammer of his Remington and sent another leaden messenger of death winging along to punch a new navel in the Mexican brigand's large, round belly.

Stale breath whooshed out of the wounded thief as he doubled over. Behind him another *ladróne* raised up to shoot at Eli. Before he could take aim on the scout, his head shattered as though from the loud belch of the .45-70 Mondragon rifle which detonated less than five feet from his right ear.

"I don't know who you are, *Señor,*" a uniformed non-com called out to Eli in Spanish, "but you are most welcome. *Cabo* Miguel Procuna at your service."

"Eli Holten," the scout answered, sensing the meaning of the introduction. "We've got us a lot of *bandidos* around here."

"There are but two of us left," Procuna went on, pointing up the car toward a sweating private. "How can we help to drive them off?"

It would be best to consolidate their forces, Eli

speculated. He pointed toward the rear of the train. "Let's go that way, Corporal, get everyone together."

Procuna understood at once. "Luis," he called to his remaining trooper. "Come this way."

Ramon daSilva had been a *bandido* since the age of fourteen. He had murdered the kindly old couple who had taken him in as a child and raised him for eight years. He stole their horse and two burros, then rode off into the mountains. Armed with a thin, long-bladed knife and a rusty old revolver that worked only occasionally, Ramon had stolen a few sheep, robbed a few fat, frightened shopkeepers of small quantities of pesos, and created a minor nuisance in a corner of the state of Zacatecas until he encountered some real bandits.

This chance acquaintance led to a new way of life for Ramon. Laughing, the hard, cruel men listened to the boy's fanciful recounting of his exploits. Then they robbed him, stripped him of all his clothes and the leader, Juan Espinosa, *El Tigre,* had spanked his bare bottom. Although humiliated and helpless, Ramon's determination did not flag. Barefoot and naked, he followed the mountain brigands. With cunning and stealth, he outfitted himself with clothing, weapons and another horse. One day he showed up in the bandit camp.

El Tigre's harshness melted away. Impressed by what the lad had accomplished, he welcomed Ramon into the gang. Now, ten years later, twenty-five-year-old Ramon daSilva held the cherished position of Number Two in the outlaw horde. He had become a vicious, brutal killer. Absolutely heartless, he mixed looting with lusty rape and bloody death. None stood in his way. While El Tigre dealt with the contents of the express car and livestock transports, Ramon led the rest of the gang in stripping the passengers of their valuables. He also compiled a short list of attractive, barely nubile females to receive his attentions once the train had been cleaned of all worth taking.

That had almost been accomplished, Ramon realized as the sound of gunfire dwindled. Stupid *soldados!* Only six of them to guard a train this size, so obviously a rich plum to be picked. Ramon had visions of going to the hot springs resort at Auguascalientes with his share of loot and living it up for a month or so. Lots of tequila, the best *putas* in town and mountains of tamales, tender quail and *carnitas*—savory, succulent chunks of pork, cooked in an open copper cauldron over a smoky wood fire. How he loved them! A sudden disturbance behind him spoiled all of Ramon's plans.

A tall *gringo* stood in the open doorway to the last car, a smoking revolver in his hand. Ramon spun to fire at him and the world turned yellow-orange before his eyes.

Missed! Eli Holten cursed his bad fortune at such short range.

Instantly, he ducked back out of the car as the heavy-set, slightly cross-eyed, bandit blazed away with a brace of nickle-plated Colts. Slugs bit into the wooden paneling of the rear wall. A shower of splinters flew from the impact. Another bullet sped through the open portal and howled off the long, solid iron shaft that ran downward from the brake wheel above. From the outside platforms between cars, the two Mexican soldiers fired at other bandits who still sat astride their horses.

Corporal Procuna scored a hit and an ugly, scar-faced outlaw uttered a soft grunt as he fell from his horse, a big

.45-70 hole in his forehead.

"Good shooting," the scout told him. A sound from above drew Eli's attention.

"If you can keep their attention, I have a grand opportunity to eliminate these *ladrónes chingados,*" Major Ocampo declared in a loud, cheerful whisper, grinning down from the roof of the car ahead. He then spoke in rapid-fire Spanish to the soldiers.

"We can do that," Eli assured him.

Cautiously, Holten edged himself closer to the open door to the last car. The muzzle of his Remington leading the way, he eased around the jam and exposed one eye.

Three frightened passengers filled the aisle. Behind them, the *bandido* squinted at the scout over a white field of excessively plentiful, slab-like teeth.

"*Ay gringo!* You choot at me an' you keel these pee-pul," Ramon daSilva grated in execrable English.

"They are of no importance to me, *tu cobardamente cabrón,*" Holten snared in return. "If they die or not makes no difference."

"*I am no coward!*" the bandit shrieked, frothy white droplets of spittal flying from his lips. "For that I shall make you suffer mightily before I keel you. *Hijo de la chingada,* I cut off your balls!"

Holten grinned nastily. "You'd like that, wouldn't you?"

Shots blasted from above them and bandits died screaming. On the vestibule, the soldiers' .45-70's opened up. More of the outlaws perished, or raced their horses away to safety. Incoherent with rage, his *machismo* unbearably insulted by this *gringo,* Ramon daSilva screamed at the scout and ran toward the door, both revolvers firing wildly.

"*Mierda in la lache de tu madre!*" the bandit howled.

Eli Holten stood to his full six-foot-one height and stepped into the open. The Remington in his right hand bucked, belching flame and smoke. Ramon daSilva came abruptly to a halt. His mouth, under its drooping wings of black mustache, formed an "Oh" as he leaned far backward. The hole in his chest began to ooze blood.

Cocked again, Holten's six-gun roared once more.

Ramon daSilva slammed backward into a dividing partition and he dropped both revolvers. Slowly his already cooling body slid down the gayly painted panel, leaving behind a shiny wet trail of red.

"He said he shit in the milk of your mother, *amigo*. In Mexico, that is a terrible insult," Major Ocampo called down from the rooftop.

"I don't think he got the chance to try it," Holten told him dryly.

Corporal Procuna and the soldier with him jumped from the train and began to fire methodically at the retreating bandits. Eli stepped out to get in a shot and saw another robber fling his arms in the air and spin to one side, as Procuna's bullet struck him in the back. The corpse bounced when it hit the ground. Eli sighted on a slow mover, who had only then exited from the express car.

A heavy bag of gold fifty-peso coins split open when struck by Eli's first bullet. Quickly the shiny circles dribbled away. Absorbed in recovering his booty, the *bandido* made no effort to defend himself. With a shrug, Holten thumbed back the hammer of his Remington and fired again.

Deprived of his golden protection, this slug punched through the empty sack and into the outlaw's chest.

There it burst his heart. He made a pair of wobbly steps, spun on one heel and flopped into a pile of horse droppings deposited by the mount of one of his fellow brigands.

"*Magnifico!*" Carlos Ocampo exclaimed. "If I am not mistaken, that was a bandit called El Tigre. Juan Espinosa was his name."

He stood upright, straddle-legged, on the top of the rearmost car. The rifle he held in his hands still smoked from his final round. With his left hand, Ocampo gestured to the litter of corpses surrounding the train.

"You are a most heroic gentleman, *Don* Eli. A fine figure of a man. Are you sure that there is no Mexican blood in your family? Wait until they hear of this in Mazatlan. There is a reward for *bandidos*, especially for El Tigre, which we will share, and the ladies will consider you most gallant. *Aye*, my friend, this will be a day that goes down in history."

Chapter 7

Carlos Ocampo's prediction proved to be quite accurate. At the *Federale's* direction, Corporal Procuna and the lone private who survived the bandit attack loaded the corpses of the outlaws aboard and inexpertly ran the train into the next major city and rail center at Culiacan. After long questioning of all four by authorities and the railroad manager, Major Ocampo filed an application for the reward with the governor and another with the railroad.

The railroad acted promptly enough. In typical fashion, though, the bureaucrats of the government moved with leaden slowness. The local officials had as yet to process the claim when a new train and crew took Eli Holten and Carlos Ocampo on to Mazatlan.

There, Carlos spared no efforts in making known the heroism of his new friend, Eli Holten. As the man who killed El Tigre, Eli found himself the invited guest of the governor, several state senators and the mayor of Mazatlan. He was wined and dined in the most elaborate of manners. After several nights of this, it began to drag on him. His enthusiasm was understandably low, then, when Carlos appeared at Eli's hotel yet again.

"Not another fancy dinner party," Eli declared through a groan. "I don't think I can handle that. Besides, I want to book my trip to La Paz tomorrow."

"No, *amigo,* not a formal affair tonight," Carlos told him laughingly. "This evening we are going to indulge in somewhat more earthly pleasures. I'm taking you to *Campo Siete.*"

"Camp Seven? What kind of pleasures can we find on an army post?"

"Eli, Eli, it's easy to see you have never been in Mazatlan before. *Campo Siete* is the—how you say?—red light district of the town."

"Whores?"

"The very same. Yes, it is time for some enduring enjoyment. Come. Be my guest. Good food, wine and women. There might even be room for a song or two."

The scout's face split in a wide grin. "You have my undivided attention."

Wildly uninhibited, *Campo Siete* turned out to be more than Deadwood City, Dodge and half a dozen more frontier sin spots combined. Quite literally, one could have anything one desired . . . for a price.

"It is him. It is the *gringo,*" people whispered as Eli and Carlos walked down the long, main street. The denizens of this city of sin jostled each other and pointed, their excited words becoming an audible ripple that preceded the pair from one establishment to another.

"No, *Señores,* it is not for you to pay. Not the man who killed El Tigre and Ramon daSilva," the bartender in a cantina named *Bajo el Cielo de Mexico* told them when Carlos ordered two tequilas with *tubos* of beer as chasers. "This is on the house."

"What's all this?" Eli inquired, thoroughly puzzled.

"Your celebrity has reached even here, *amigo,*" Carlos told him. "You are a hero of Mexico now. I wouldn't be surprised if you didn't receive offers of some more, ah, intimate rewards before the night is over."

"Here? From working whores? Not very likely, Carlos. Better chance they'd double the price, seein's how I'm so well known."

Carlos joined in the scout's laughter. The *cantinero* brought their drinks. Carlos hoisted his tall, straight-sided shotglass of tequila and tipped the rim toward Eli. "*Salud, dinero y amor . . . y tiempo de gustarlos.*"

They drained their crystal-clear shots of fiery tequila and swallowed down half of the long, slender glass of beer that came with it. Eli smacked his lips and wiped away a frothy mustache of foam with the back of his left hand.

"That toast . . . what does it mean in English?"

"Health, money and love . . . and time to enjoy them all."

"Hell, that just about says everything worth saying."

"You have the right of it there, *amigo.* Come. Finish your beer and we'll go to this place I have in mind. *Ay de mí,* you won't believe it. There is this girl there, she must have the biggest pussy ever. She . . . now, this is really the truth . . . she actually takes on a burro right there on the stage. Him with his *cholo* dragging the ground and she takes in every inch. *Que magnifico.*"

"*Que* disgusting," the scout returned. "What does she do, tickle it with her tonsils while he's humping away?"

Carlos affected a serious, contemplative expression. "You know, I never thought of that before."

"To tell you the truth, Carlos, I've always been more

of a doer than a watcher. Spectator sports are for those who are unwilling, or unable, to participate."

Ocampo made big eyes. "Oh-ho, then. I have exactly the perfect place for you, *amigo*. Hurry. Drink your *cerveza* and we go. It's called *Club la Taberna*. You'll like it, I guarantee."

He did, Eli discovered only moments after they entered the establishment. Two comely young ladies walked toward them, hips swiveling in a seductive sway. Clearly, they were the most attractive women Eli had seen all evening. He felt a familiar stirring in his loins as he inhaled the heady perfume worn by the one who singled him out.

"You are a handsome man, *Señor*," she murmured in Spanish.

Holten's facility with the language had been improving steadily and he appreciated the ring of sincerity behind the commercial compliment. "Thank you. You're quite adorable," he responded.

A genuine smile brightened her face. She had classic features, Eli decided. Aztec or some other aristocratic tribe from before the conquistadors. A high forehead, large, wide-spaced eyes and a proud prow of slightly arched nose enlivened her dusky skin and blended with a generous, full-lipped mouth. She had small ears, that peeped out from behind rich, raven tresses. Coyly, she placed a hand on his chest.

"You are the famous *gringo* who fought the bandits on the train from Hermosillo, *verdad?*"

Accustomed to the fact that his exaggerated exploits had penetrated into this city-within-a-city, her statement still surprised the scout. He blinked his eyes and made a deprecating gesture.

"As my friend, Carlos, here said, I could get just as dead in Mexico as in my own country, so I did what had to be done."

"You are too modest, *Señor.*"

"I'm . . ." Eli searched for the word, "unused to flattery."

"Not flattery, *Señor* Holten. Notoriety. You are famous now. Many men have died trying to do what you did. It took courage, strength and skill. And I can see that you're *muy guapo!* Every bit a man, I'm sure."

"Uh . . . thank you again. It seems you know my name, but I'm not acquainted with yours."

"I am called Alicia. But my name is really Juanita. Juanita Valdez. And may I call you Eli? I . . . have a place where I can entertain . . . certain special friends. Would you like to go there with me?"

"Would I like it?" The offer astounded him. Carlos had been right. Eli also realized that he couldn't think of a better idea. A well-known swelling began in his loins.

"Juanita, that's the best offer I've had all night. I would more than *like* . . . I . . . uh, insist. Take me away from all this. Show me a garden of delights."

Juanita made a warm, rumbling sound deep in her throat. "For you, Eli, it would be my pleasure. I will certainly show you my *jardin de la encantares.*"

On the way to her private abode, Juanita made it clear that this was not a professional engagement. "This is between a man and a woman, you and I, and a matter of unbridled passion," she whispered in his ear.

Inside the small house, Juanita poured wine, a rather good vintage from the mountains of Central Mexico.

Eli sipped it appreciatively. He was, by far, not a connoisseur, but the fresh, crisp taste appealed to him. Juanita refilled his glass and he reached out to draw her down onto his lap.

She felt the rigid bulk of him even through the thick material of her dress. Her eyes widened with anticipation and she kissed him on the nose. One of Eli's big hands cupped a breast and he began to tease the nipple with thumb and forefinger. Juanita toyed with a curly lock of Holten's dusty blond hair. Holten slid his other paw up under the hem of Juanita's dress and gently squeezed her warm thigh. Juanita sighed.

With consummate ease and familiarity, Eli began to undress her. Her stiff, satiny outer garment came away in a single piece once the hook-eye fasteners had been undone. It rustled like dry Fall leaves as she stood in one smooth motion and shucked it. Before Eli could continue his exploration, she stepped away and lowered the wicks of the two brass lamps that illuminated the whitewashed plaster walls. She returned with arms outstretched.

"It is time to stroll through that garden," Juanita declared as she executed a graceful pirouette.

"With the greatest of pleasure," the scout assured her.

He bent and lifted the soft cotton fabric of her shift. It rose slowly, revealing her silky, light-tan legs and thighs. Only the scantest few wispy black threads adorned the swollen halves of her vertically cleft mound. Moisture glistened in the pink pout of her treasure trove and a thrill of excitement coarsed through Eli's firm, muscular body. Higher he lifted the simple frock until he gazed at the small dimple of her perfectly round navel, set against the slight swell of a taut abdomen. Further, still, the arched flare of her ribcage brought new surges of delight to the avid observer.

Eli's hand trembled slightly as he revealed small, pert breasts, the dark circles of the areolas puffy and distended, nipples swelling as his gaze brushed over them. His throbbing organ of generation ached at the restraint of his clothing. Shyly, Juanita reached out and laid her warm little hand on the bulge in Eli's fine-weave woolen trousers.

"*Ay, es muy grande,*" Juanita breathed heavily.

Eli leaned forward and kissed her belly. Juanita wriggled under the caress of his lips and felt a jolt of sheer joy flash through her fine-tuned body. She undid his tie and pulled his white linen shirt from his waistband. Freed, she quickly removed it and gasped at the sight of so many scars on his lightly bronzed body. Most particularly her eyes were drawn to the close-spaced vertical red marks above each nipple, where his skin had been loosened for the wooden plugs of the Sun Dance. Gently she traced them with a fingertip.

"What caused these?" she inquired in a tiny voice.

"It is difficult to explain in a language I am only learning. They were done by the Sioux Indians for the ritual of the Sun Dance. Wooden plugs are inserted and rawhide tied to the ends. You must dance until the skin tears and you fall to the ground."

"A torture?"

"No. A . . . religious thing."

"*Los indios?* I am Indian, too. But I am a Catholic. We do not afflict ourselves with such terrible things to please God."

"It is their way."

"Then why did you make yourself go through it?"

"I . . . it was necessary. And that is the hard part to explain."

Eli stood suddenly and undid the string fastenings of his beltless trousers. Juanita squealed with rapture when his long, fat maleness swung upward from its furry nest and swayed before her. Eagerly, she reached out and encircled the silken flesh with warm, moist fingers.

"Never. Never before have I seen so . . . so much of a man," she ardently declared. "All others are as small boys to you, my precious Eli."

Juanita sank to her knees and opened her lush lips. With studied languor, she extended her tongue and inscribed spirals on the fiery tip of his masterful possession. She bent further forward, sending twitters of jubilation along its rigid staff as she cupped the smooth, hot flesh and enclosed it in her tugging, pulsing mouth. Bit by bit she ingested all she could contain. Eli vibrated like a plucked violin string. With single-minded purpose she began to work back and forth, forcing even more of the sweet-tasting rod into the steamy depths of her welcoming throat.

She began to hum and the vibrations did spectacular things to the raw nerve endings of his engorged phallus. Deeper she went and a moan escaped from Eli's tightly clinched lips. Another violent thrust and her Aztec lips nuzzled in the thick thatch of reddish-yellow hair that surrounded the base of his rock-hard machine. He began to pant and to moan and his hips flexed of their own accord while lightning bolts of excruciatingly wonderful pleasure pierced his being.

Then he could contain his emotions no longer. With

an anguished cry, he unleashed a burning stream of his nectar and sagged weakly as Juanita continued to lap at his still-rigid manhood. As though in a dream, Eli reached down to her.

Eli raised Juanita by the shoulders to full height and kissed her hard on the mouth. A groan escaped from deep in his chest, testimony to the intensity of his need.

He pressed his torrid flesh against her naked body and an electric shock stuttered along his nerves as the burning tip of his engorged phallus drove into the softness of her belly. Juanita had not released her hold on his pulsing manhood and now she bent it downward until the thick tip parted the leafy portals of her chamber and came to rest against the distended node of sublime joy that tingled at his touch.

Starbursts exploded in both their heads as Eli ground his manly lance against the seething button and Juanita quavered with ecstacy. He flexed his knees, slid his massive member lower and then, with a gulp and a moan, he impaled her.

Juanita's feet came off the floor and she locked her ankles behind Eli's narrow, bony waist. He cupped her buttocks in both massive hands and began to drive his lengthy shaft deep within her tightly contracting passage. Juanita squeaked and howled, pounded tiny, ineffectual fists against his broad, hard chest and thrashed her head from side to side, transported by the heavenly friction of unquestionably the largest male organ she had ever encountered. With each stroke, Eli's frenzy grew.

Little yelps of pleasure came from Juanita, and the scout heard himself responding with grunts and plaintive whimpers. He slowed his pace as the staggering paroxysms of untrammeled bliss escalated toward the ultimate detonation. Juanita began to shudder with great convulsions, and Eli plowed into her with renewed vigor so that they burst asunder into the excrescent oblivion of mutual dissolution.

And to think, Eli purred happily in his swirling mind as he carried her toward the bed, the night had only begun.

Chapter 8

From the pages of *Hoy* and *Noticias de Mazatlan,* headlines proclaimed the fighting in Baja California. The usually crowded ticket office of the ferry company echoed emptily when Eli Holten entered the next morning. He walked a bit stiff-legged and a pleasant ache radiated from his loins. He had left Juanita's small house in *Campo Siete* only minutes after sunrise and taken a burro-drawn cab back into town.

At his hotel, he had shaved and dressed in fresh clothes, then packed his belongings and made arrangements for his Morgan stallion, Sonny, to be prepared for the ship passage to the Baja Peninsula. After an early breakfast, Holten went directly to the bayside building that housed the ferry company.

"*Quero una pasaje para viaje a La Paz, por favor,*" Eli said in careful Spanish.

Startled by the unusual accent, the vendor shot a suspicious glance upward at the scout, lips pursed in contemplation. "Passage to La Paz? It is not safe to go there, *Señor.*"

"I realize that. But I must go anyway. I'll also need a stall for my horse."

"The next ferry does not sail until tomorrow."

"I know that, too. Now may I please have a ticket?" Holten's patience had begun to fray at the edges.

"Ah . . . *sí, Señor*. If you will wait a moment." The ticket seller rose and hurried away from the grill that separated his booth from the public.

What the hell is that all about? the scout wondered.

A minute later he found out as the ferry agent returned with two policemen. The lawmen approached with purposeful strides, hands on the butts of their Fabrica Mendoza copies of the Model '73 Colts that they wore high on their hips in basket-weave, hand-tooled leather holsters.

"There he is. The *gringo mercenario*. Arrest him!" the ticket merchant shouted, aquiver with agitation.

Awh, shit, the scout thought. Of all the people in this town who had heard over and over about his exploits on the train, this one had to be the only person who didn't know him by sight. Eli raised a hand in a peaceful gesture.

"Hey, wait a minute. He's made a mistake. I'm Eli Holten, the one who fought the bandits on the train from Hermosillo."

"We know of no bandits, *Señor* Holten. You will come with us, *Señor*," the larger policeman with the bay-window belly declared in a hard, flat voice.

"No, I won't. I'm not one of Madonna's invaders. But I do have information that may help stop them."

"You are going to jail, *Señor*. Your Spanish is very good, if a bit limited," the big one added a left-handed compliment. "Even so, we cannot have more foreign *ladrónes* invading Baja California. Come peacefully or we will use force."

"Ooh, *damnit!*" Eli exclaimed.

It would be useless to resist. He knew that only too well. Any such action would be seen as proof of the accusation. He shrugged mightily and stepped toward the lawmen. Instantly, the short, skinny one drew his revolver.

"Take it easy. I'm doing what you say. Do one thing for me, though, will you? Contact Major Carlos Ocampo of the *Federales.* He's staying at *la Posada de Sinaloa.* Tell him that you have Eli Holten in jail and why. He'll vouch for me."

"Oh, *sí, sí.* I'm sure you know a number of *Federales,* but not as friends, I'll wager," Eli's beer-belly captor rumbled, a tinkle of amusement in his voice. "You will surrender your sidearm, please, and come with us."

The palm-thatch roof of the small farmhouse ahead lifted off and sailed away. Myron Henshaw saw it happen. Even so, he didn't quite believe it.

"What kind of storm is this?" he shouted at Iron Mike Madonna over the tumult of the wind.

"Hurricane. They're rather common along the West Coast of Mexico. Even more so here on the peninsula."

"Do they get any worse?"

"Oh, yes. Much." Iron Mike looked off to the west, where boiling charcoal gray and funereal black clouds had lowered to the heaving, green-gray surface of the sea. "We have maybe half an hour. We'll hole up in Pasaje de los Reyes."

A blinding curtain of gigantic raindrops swept down and obscured the distant ocean, seen only sporadically through the broken passes in the mountains. Iron Mike's army moved soddenly along the muddy track. A heavy mist fell on them and none of the adventurers contemplated the rapidly approaching torrent of the hurricane with pleasure.

"Do you figure there'll be any delay in taking the town?"

Iron Mike snorted. "Hell no. It's only a little mountain village. Maybe one lawdog if they have any at all. Chances are that, outside of a few shotguns, nobody will be armed. We'll just move in and take over. Then we can sit out the storm."

Henshaw shivered involuntarily. The bull-roar of the wind bothered him. It reminded him of the tornadoes he had seen on the Great Plains. A brutal, mindless force of nature that ripped and tore its way across flatlands, mountains or water seemed to him to be ample proof that no kind and loving Diety looked over the affairs of man.

How puny are our greatest efforts in the face of such devastation, he thought as he looked warily at the approaching hurricane. He cast a glance to his right where Constance Williams rode in silence, swathed in a native poncho. A large sombrero drooped on her head, water dripping from its wide, up-turned brim. For the first time Myron could recall, she had a bedraggled appearance. A tenderness toward her rekindled, to be shattered by her words, which matched her recent assertiveness.

"I feel like something the birds have been shitting on," Connie declared as she wiped away a trickle of rainwater that ran down her neck.

Behind them a horse whinnied in panic as a powerful gust of wind rocked it nearly off its feet. Myron and Constance tight-reined their own mounts to prevent the alarm from spreading.

"You're picking up some bad habits from these soldiers," Myron observed.

"Piss on that," Connie growled. "Did I ever tell you how I lost my virtue at thirteen? After that, I couldn't get enough cock. George fucked me regularly enough for the next two years, until his company moved him to another town. Even with that, I was hot for it all the time. Big or little, I didn't care, so long as they could get it stiff and poke it in me. Trouble was, I was scared of being caught. So I never had all I wanted. I tried, though, and I learned some mighty rough language in the process.

"Maybe being with Iron Mike's army, watching people die, women get raped, has made me revert to type."

"That's nonsense, Connie," Myron protested, touched by her recounting. "You're refined, well-read. A real lady. Yessir, that's what I thought the first time I met you. I've not had cause to think otherwise since. You're a wildcat in bed, but that don't take away from your lady-like qualities. This is no place for a woman. It's had . . . an influence on you."

Constance laughed harshly. "All bad, I'm sure you see it. God! When are we going to get out of this horrible storm?"

"Soon now. It had better be or we'll go flying away like that roof."

"That made my blood run cold," Constance admitted. "I've never seen weather so terrible. How far to Pasaje de los Reyes?"

"Three miles, maybe four. Iron Mike said we'd make it in a little less than half an hour at this pace."

"Mud!" Constance said it like a curse. "I hope I never see mud again."

Seemingly in defiance of Constance's declaration, a

large protrusion of the mountainside pulled away with a sucking sound and plopped noisily down on the trail. Horses skittered nervously, wickering and rolling their eyes until mostly white showed. Constance's mount side-stepped nervously around the mudslide and rippled its hide in distaste. How could a desert, and that's surely what they were in, produce so much mud? Not finding an answer, Constance worried the question as the long column continued its slow, steady advance.

Twenty minutes later the gunfire echoed along the curve of the mountain. A rider spurred back from the three-man point. When he neared, he swept his hat from his head and began to swing it in wide circles.

"There was only two of them!" the freebooter shouted. "We got 'em both. The town is ours."

He reined in with a spray of mud and sloppily saluted Iron Mike. "It was some hick lawman with a rusty old Colt and the mayor with a shotgun. They knew who we were and told us that Pasaje de los Reyes would never surrender. Hell, it was easy, Mike. While the mayor was still jabberin' away, we just shot 'em both full of holes."

The rain had become a regular deluge and the world had been restricted to a gray haze only a few yards across. Wind, far exceeding gale force, lashed the drops sideways so that they assaulted everyone horizontally. Iron Mike took a long look at this and made a sweeping arm gesture forward.

"Let's pick up the pace. That damned hurricane isn't gonna wait for us."

"I wonder what it would feel like to be dry for a change?" Constance speculated aloud.

The last of the heavy caissons of the artillery had just

entered through the wide doors of a large storage loft a block off the plaza in Pasaje de los Reyes when the hurricane struck with its full strength.

The few glass windows in town bulged outward, then exploded into the rooms as enormous pressure changes alternated in the roaring, shrieking storm. Even the sturdy, three-foot thick adobe walls of the buildings trembled as blasts of wind, moving in excess of a hundred thirty miles an hour, savaged them. Flying sand and small cacti scoured the whitewash off exteriors and eroded away the surfaces of wooden support posts. In the belfry of the church, the big brass tocsins clanged insanely. The terrified populace huddled together in their homes and prayed.

In what had been the home of the murdered mayor, Constance Williams crouched, too, hugging her knees tight to her chest beside a cold fireplace. Several fires had started when tumultuous gusts had blown down chimneys and scattered blazing coals and showers of sparks throughout rooms filled with highly flammable materials. Iron Mike had ordered all hearthfires extinguished to prevent more. Outside, the tempest hovered over the small mountain town and hurled its worst excesses against the frail conceits of man.

Discordant and flat, church bells near the jail sounded the quarter hours. A carillon joined in at the half hour, and on the hour, an even deader tocsin tolled out the count. Eli Holten had counted forty of these out-of-tune chimings since being deprived of all his possessions and unceremoniously dumped into a flagstone-floored cell.

His prison smelled of vomit and stale urine. The damp stone walls exuded moisture, which had rusted the bars in many places, so that the gray paint covering them had become scabrous. As though afflicted with some iron-corrupting pox, Eli reflected sourly. Only open bars separated the cages in a long row. Scant light came through small, narrow windows set high in the wall on the opposite side of the corridor. Through them, he saw thin slices of blue day, darkening now as night lowered over Mazatlan. He had not eaten since breakfast and his stomach rumbled in complaint.

A vendor had come around at noon, selling tamales, tacos and ears of roast corn. Eli had not been allowed to keep any money. The savory odors had lingered with him through half of the afternoon. It did little for his comfort or peace of mind. Where was Carlos? Had the police even contacted him?

Somehow, Holten doubted it.

A jarring clank came from the bells, announcing quarter after seven. Eli winced at the metallic cacophony. Much longer, he considered, and he'd be talking to himself like the drooling old man in the cell next to his.

Down the way, a group of street waifs sat in a circle, masturbating and wagering copper pesos on who would ejaculate first. Next to them, a man who had been savagely beaten by the police moaned and turned restlessly in semi-consciousness.

Up the other direction, nearest to the solid, heavy iron door to the cellblock, two drunks argued incoherently over whose fault it had been the police arrested them. Where the hell was Carlos? Eli's ribs and shoulders ached from where he had been routinely pounded by night sticks, wielded by the fat policeman and his skinny companion.

If it was the last thing he did, the scout promised himself, he would get out of this jail and look up that pair. Then he'd take his time, wringing the little one's turkey neck and kicking the puss-gutted lawman's ass up between his shoulder blades.

Chapter 9

Doves ruffled their feathers and cooed sweetly from the narrow, barred windows of the Mazatlan jail. The scene would have been almost tranquil, Eli Holten thought, if those damned bells hadn't started up again. The slop that had been served for supper still remained in a congealed mass on the tin plate he had set aside the previous night.

No one had come to pick it up and the scout wondered if the jailers would bring breakfast. The speculation didn't please him. They just might do it. Huge alabaster clouds had begun to billow off to the west, blocking some of the radiant blue of the tropical sky. Down the corridor, the street urchins yelled shrilly as two of their number started a fight. Eli began to pace his cell.

He'd made only three turns when the big door at the nearer end slammed open and two figures entered. Behind them came a trustee, pushing a wooden-wheeled cart on which sat a steaming cauldron.

"Eli! *Amigo,* where are you?" a familiar voice called out.

"Carlos!" the scout shouted. He could hardly believe his good fortune.

"*Ay de mí!* You look terrible. You don't belong here,

you know. I've arranged for your release. The officers who arrested you are most sorry for the mistake," Carlos went on as he stepped close to the barred front of Eli's cell.

"I'd like to make them a little sorrier," Holten growled.

"Once I learned what had happened, I sent four of my *Federales* to convince them of the error of their ways. They, ah, will not be working for a few days."

Holten's laughter echoed off the walls. It stopped the fight among the small boys, who watched big-eyed as the turnkey unlocked Eli's cell and stepped aside.

"He is yours, *Señor Mayor,*" the warden announced to Carlos. His tone held considerable deference and respect.

"Thank you, Sanchez. Your cooperation will be remembered. Now, come, Eli. We have time for breakfast and conversation before your ferry sails." Carlos eyed the cart as it rolled by, a malevolent odor rising from the contents of the kettle.

"I thought it wise to get you out of here before they served what passes for, ah, food around this place."

"A brilliant decision," Eli acknowledged. "I'll settle for a bath first, if it can be arranged."

"Easily." Carlos reached upward and placed an arm around Eli's shoulder. Chatting cordially, he guided the scout out of the *carcel.*

Forty minutes later, Eli emerged from a public bath house, refreshed, smelling slightly of oil of roses, his day's growth of stubble shaved off and hair slicked back. He had dressed in a lightweight daytime suit and enjoyed the welcoming comfort around his waist of the wide cartridge belt that held his holstered Remington revolver.

Carlos clapped his big American friend on the back. "Now for a big bowl of *menudo* and a plate of *enchiladas suiza.*"

"What's *menudo?*" Eli asked.

"A soup made of hominy, onions, chili peppers, calves feet and beef tripes. Delicious! The world's greatest hangover cure, my friend. And don't tell me that after a night in jail you don't feel like you have the all-time greatest headache."

Eli had to laugh, despite the residual discomfort that put the truth to Carlos' words. The *Federale* major directed them to a waterfront restaurant, where huge, steaming bowls of *menudo* were brought to their table. The scout looked at the condiment tray that accompanied the soup; chopped fresh corriander, dried oregano leaves, diced chili peppers, lemon halves and fresh onion and decided to follow Carlos' lead.

The thick, flavorful broth turned out to be delicious. The two men ate in animated silence, occasional murmurs of appreciation escaping them. When Eli finished the last drop in his bowl, it was whisked away and the waiter brought large platters of shredded beef enchiladas, smothered in cheese and topped with a piquant red sauce and two fried eggs.

"Any time they want to dish out food like this in that jail, I'll be happy to stay there," Eli remarked as he pressed the side of his fork into a tender roll of corn tortilla filled with meat and onions.

"Our *carcels* are intended to punish, not to provide every luxury. Is it not so in your country?"

"Yes, it is," Eli readily agreed. "If the purpose ever changes, though, we'll be in for a lot of trouble."

Eli and Carlos reached the ferry slip an hour later. The

Federale displayed a ticket and smiled at Eli's surprise.

"I decided to come along. After all, it might be you need an influential voice again, no?"

Carlos had arranged in advance for his horse and Eli's Sonny to be taken aboard. All that remained was for them to climb the gangplank and locate their quarters. It turned out that a small stateroom in the deckhouse had been arranged for the ranking federal policeman and his American companion. While they settled in, the order came to make sail and slip free the moorings.

"It is a two day trip, since the prevailing winds are against us crossing the Sea of Cortez," Carlos explained to Eli. "But at least we have an off-shore breeze to aid us out of the bay."

The deck lurched under them as wind filled the canvas aloft. Never having developed sea-legs, Eli stumbled and caught himself against the raised rail of his bunk. Through the porthole, he saw the shore slipping past and away. The pitch and roll of the ship made the usually solid, verdant hillsides of palm, cypress and patchwork fields appear to oscillate. Eli viewed the phenomenon with a landman's typical trepidation.

"I have called you gentlemen here because we are faced with considerable difficulty," Captain Ramon Garcia of the *Riena del Pacifico* informed Eli Holten and Carlos Ocampo shortly before noon of the next day.

"The weather is worsening with each passing hour. Our glass is falling rapidly," the captain went on. "We have come too far to turn back and outrun the storm. It is a *chirabusco.* A hurricane. There were no indications before we left Mazatlan. Now . . ." Captain Garcia shrugged expressively.

"I'm no sailor," the scout began, "but I thought the water was getting a little rough. What will this hurricane mean to us?"

"We have two choices. The one we pick can mean survival . . . or tragedy."

"Can you explain that a little more thoroughly, Captain?" Carlos requested.

"We can continue on this long southward tack and run as far in toward the peninsula as we can, or we can try to sail northward out of the path of the storm. Both courses offer difficulties."

"Such as?" Eli pressed.

"If we continue on this tack, we will be forced to go about and run with the storm when the hurricane hits us full force. Otherwise we would be swamped. The result would be at least an additional day's sailing to reach La Paz. Going north is a long gamble since there is no way of predicting the path taken by the *chirabusco.* If it veers northward with us, which many hurricanes do, it could hit us broadside and overturn the vessel."

"Not a cheery prospect either way," Eli observed. "What is it we're supposed to do?"

Garcia smiled tightly and brushed at his full mustache. "Call it moral support, *Señor.* I only wished to advise you of our alternatives and ask that you back me in my decision."

"Which is?"

Again Garcia shrugged. "In clear conscience, I can only determine that we will be safer by maintaining our present course."

"Well then, that's it, no?" Carlos remarked with a forced casualness.

An hour later, visibility had been reduced to only a few feet beyond the bowsprit. The *Riena del Pacifico* traveled under small sail, which the captain ordered further shortened to storm sails only, as the wind gusted to greater speed and mountainous waves hurtled down on the plunging ship. The howling tempest shrieked through the rigging and two stays parted with sharp reports like gunshots, their wrist-thick lengths streaming away sternward, like threads in a breeze.

"Prepare to ware ship!" the captain shouted above the fury.

"All hands on deck. Make ready to come about!" the boatswain bellowed.

Bare feet thudded on the deck, inaudible in the raging hurricane. Many passengers had become violently seasick. Eli Holten felt gratitude that he, at least, didn't appear to suffer from the malady. In the cargo hold laid out for livestock, the horses and mules screamed in terror and rolled large, white eyes. When the hands had manned their stations, Captain Garcia gave the order to turn the ship around so that they could run with the storm.

Captain Garcia's determination to gain all the westward distance possible had severely endangered the *Riena del Pacifico.* Gigantic green waves crashed over the bow and poured into below deck areas, drawning the vessel deeper into the water. The pumps ran constantly, completely unable to keep up with the tremendous seas that blasted aboard. As the ship slowly heeled and began to come about, the full might of the hurricane struck with devastating power.

More stays parted and their bite ends struck down seamen, who fell shrieking into the hostile water that frothed and foamed around the fragile wooden vessel. The masts began to creak ominously and jitter in their steppings. More lines parted and the mizzenmast began to gyrate wildly. A topman sent aloft to shorten sail wailed piteously when he became dislodged and hurtled to his death on the heaving deck below. The *Riena del Pacifico* lurched and staggered and began to roll far over as the monstrous waves struck broadside.

"Faster! Faster!" the captain screamed. "Hard aport!"

"Eight feet of water in the bilges, Captain, and rising," the second officer announced. "We're taking it on too fast for the pumps to handle. A little more and it'll flood the holds."

"We've got to lighten the ship," Captain Garcia decided aloud.

Eli Holten grasped a safety line from the deckhouse to the quarter deck and pulled himself along, inundated by cataclysmic wave after wave. Fighting to keep his footing, he reached the short three-step ladder to the quarter deck. With the strength of both arms he heaved himself upward.

"Is there anything we can do to help?" he inquired of the captain.

"We have to lighten the load. The ship's taking on too much water. There are some carts and other deck cargo. Join the men who are cutting them free and throwing them overside."

"Right."

With a splintering crack, which had been preceded only a fraction of a second by a sound resembling a thunderclap, the mizzenmast sheered off some twelve feet above the waist of the ship. The huge shaft of oak slammed violently into the deck, sending up showers of splinters. It tottered briefly, then hurtled over one side, smashing the brightly painted taffrail and crushing the lapstrake gunwhale. Three men howled in anguish, pierced in several parts of their bodies by flying shards of hull planks.

"Cut it away! Cut it away!" Captain Garcia bellowed.

Eli Holten joined the men working frantically to cut free the massive wooden column of the mast and let it slide away into the sea. He grabbed up an axe and began to hack at tangled knots of rigging. Salt spray stung his eyes and the furor of the hurricane sucked the breath from his mouth. Creeks and groans accompanied his effort. Around him, men labored in a frenzy.

Chapter 10

When the gunners tried to get their first field piece on the road again, it sank hub-deep in grainy, viscous mud. The hurricane had stalled against the mountains for half a day, battering at the walls of Pasaje de los Reyes, then continued its advance. A whole day of light, but continuous downpour passed before the back edge of the gigantic storm cell slid off to the east and the rain stopped. Even so, the night went by under dark and threatening clouds. Dawn of the third day since the hurricane came in gray murk, though the sky to the west showed a bright, pristine blue. Iron Mike Madonna ordered the advance to continue.

The small mountain village had nothing to offer in the way of loot or recruits. Ahead lay El Triunfo and the silver mines. As captain of the free company, Madonna chaffed to get to the reward that would keep the men loyal to him. The silver ingots beckoned to him. Only the mud defeated him.

"We'll be here a good three days," he complained to Ed Robbins, his second in command. "Damn this mud."

"It's still desert, Mike. Give it a day or so and this'll all drain off."

"Hummph!" Iron Mike grumped. "You're right, of course, but any delay now is costing us. Have the men round up all the food supplies in town. Beans, rice, corn especially, things that will keep. And have those artillerymen get that damned twelve pounder out of the mud."

Shortly after noon, three men rode into town. They were splendidly dressed in tight-fitting trousers and waist-length jackets of matching color. Each had crossed bandoliers of ammunition on their chests and their dark, mustachioed faces were shaded by huge, wide-brimmed sombreros. Embroidered white shirts, frilly, colorful cravats and high-top, shiny boots completed their costumes. They looked straight ahead as they walked their mounts to the plaza. There they halted and the one slightly ahead of the other two called out in a voice at once quiet, though commanding.

"Who is in charge here?"

Robbins, who spoke excellent Spanish, answered, "Iron Mike Madonna. We are a free company, seeking to establish a small state of our own. Who are you?"

"I am called Pedro Encino. I've come to offer the services of myself and my men."

"You are bandits?" Robbins asked.

Encino chuckled softly. "Let us say that, like you, we are adventurers."

"I . . . see. Well, then, if you will dismount and refresh yourselves in the cantina over there, I'll have Iron Mike brought to you."

"You are most kind. *Andele, muchachos,*" he added as he swung a leg over the ornate Spanish saddle and dropped lightly to the ground.

Although excited by the prospect that some of the local

bandits had at last decided to make contact, Iron Mike Madonna waited a calculated twenty minutes before walking casually to the door of the cantina, from his command post across the plaza. He entered and walked directly to the table where three men scowled their impatience at the delay.

"*Señor* Encino?" Iron Mike inquired of the trio.

"I am Pedro Encino," a tall, lean man, darkest of the three declared.

"*Con mucho gusto, Don* Pedro," Madonna responded. "I am Captain Madonna. I understand from my adjutant that you and your men seek to join our expedition. Is that correct?"

"*Exactamente.* Provided of course . . . that the terms of our association will be mutually beneficial." Encino's icy smile could have cut diamonds.

Iron Mike frowned slightly, then extended both hands, palms up, in a placating gesture. He used his most conciliatory tone as he told the bandit chieftain the hard facts.

"I have nearly five hundred men under my command. Half a dozen artillery pieces. We have had few losses. You command what? Say thirty to forty ill-equipped and undisciplined hill marauders. We have artillerymen, grenadiers, cavalry. Surely you can see that joining us in order to stay alive and earn an equal share in the booty should be of sufficient 'mutual' benefit."

"And the alternative, Captain?"

"I'll put it simply for you. In a word—extermination. We will have enough difficulty holding what we conquer from outside assaults by the Mexican army. We cannot tolerate internal opposition as well." The ready smile came back. "So then, do we have an agreement?"

Encino swallowed hard. "I had thought to propose a partnership."

"I am captain of a free company. All who follow me are subordinate. You are either for us or against us. If you were to ride into Todos Santos, Santiago or Cabo San Lucas, you would see the penalty for opposing that simple chain of command."

Silence held for a long, tense moment, as Pedro Encino brushed at his drooping mustache with the big knuckle of his right index finger. He and his men had been in Todos Santos. *Madre de Dios* such destruction! Rape, murder, looting . . . and the town nearly flattened by artillery fire. These *gringos* had done this. He might be a bandit, but he loved his country. For Mexico and freedom, he swore to find a way to foil this foreign invasion of his beloved nation. Part of his plan included joining the freebooters.

"You are most persuasive, *Capítan,*" Pedro boomed, in a voice he hoped sounded suitably cowed and warmly sincere. "Your arguments carry considerable, ah, conviction. My men and I know these mountains like the hairs of our mustaches. Perhaps if we acted as a company of scouts and advance patrols, we would be of the most service to you?"

Iron Mike studied on the offer. It could prove valuable. He nodded and a genuine smile appeared. "An excellent idea, *Don* Pedro. Of course, a few of my men could be attached, so they could become familiar with the terrain?" It had been a statement, rather than a question.

"*Naturalamente.*"

"Yes, it might well work out, then."

"We are agreed?"

"Agreed." Iron Mike rose and extended a hand to be shaken.

Hating the *gringo,* Pedro Encino stood to his full height and clasped hands. Then he swallowed his repugnance enough to give the foreigner an *abarazo.*

"We await your orders, *mí Capítan,*" Encino declared smartly, clicking the heels of his high boots.

Their efforts began to tell, Holten discovered, as the mast made a sudden lurch to one side. His back ached and his arms felt like lead bars. Mechanically he had continued to swing the axe for a wild fifteen minutes. He took another swipe at a tightly stretched hauser and the keen blade bit through the braided strands of hemp. A loud screech of protest could barely be heard over the fury of the hurricane.

"Look out!" the seaman next to him cried.

"She's going!"

Dropping the axe, Eli leaped away as the whole weight of the mast shifted and hurtled over the side.

White spume boiled around the huge length of the mizzenmast as it struck the water. Swiftly, driven by the raging sea, it slipped away astern. Holten remembered the earlier suggestion of the captain and hurried forward to help with lightening the ship.

Crewmen stood about in somewhat confusion, only a few of them working effectively. Quickly the scout's shouted instructions organized their efforts.

"Cut those ropes, heave the carts over the side. Canvas and all. Hurry."

At first it seemed to have no effect. Then gradually,

imperceptibly, the bow began to rise. Less of the hissing green water crashed above the bowsprit and hurtled down on deck. The *Riena del Pacifico* responded to her rudder and the forepeak continued to box the compass as it swung further out of the teeth of the tempest.

"That's it!" Eli shouted in encouragement. "Throw all that cargo over."

"Stop it! Stop that!"

A short, fat man with large graying sideburns appeared suddenly on deck, waving his arms and shouting. He wore an expensive suit of clothes, black, high button shoes and a sodden hat which he clutched at now as the roaring wind threatened to rip it from his head. He rushed forward to where Eli helped jettison cargo.

"You can't do that! That's my property you're destroying."

"You'd rather go down with the ship?" Eli yelled back at him.

Ignoring the scout, the portly merchant turned toward one of the seamen and began to pound on his muscular shoulders with small, ineffectual fists. Holten reached him in two strides. The scout's huge hand flashed out and jerked the frantic little man around.

"Quit that, you fool! If this stuff doesn't go over the side, we'll founder. Captain's orders are to dispose of it. If you want to shout at someone, go find him. We haven't the time."

"But . . . but . . . I'll be ruined!" the wild-eyed businessman wailed, pounding Holten's chest.

Eli backhanded him. The small man's head snapped to one side. "That's preferable to being deader than your old emperor, Maximilian, isn't it?"

Black eyes blinked at Holten's remark and the chubby

little passenger calmed slightly. Blood oozed from a split lip. A groan escaped him as four burly deckhands tipped another cart over the rail.

"Ruined . . . ruined," he muttered plaintively as he tottered off drunkenly.

Waves no longer crashed over the bow. Much of the rage of the hurricane had ceased to pound at the sodden men at the forepeak. The *Riena del Pacifico* leaped forward, riding the crest of the gigantic combers, rather than crashing into them, as she settled on a new course, running with the tempest. Holten worked his way toward the quarterdeck once more.

"What can I do now?" Eli inquired of Captain Garcia.

"See what's needed below decks. Major Ocampo is already down there."

"Right, Captain." Eli paused before attempting the short ladder again. "The storm seems to be letting up some," he remarked.

"It's the eye. Hurricanes all have a peaceful area at their center. It could be half a league in size, or much smaller. Perhaps even larger. There is no way of telling. There the winds fall off and the water is calm. It is only an illusion, though. On the other side, the storm is often worse than the leading edge."

"That sounds so encouraging," Eli remarked dryly as he started down to the ship's waist.

Eli found Carlos one deck below, with the second and third class passengers. The low, close quarters reeked of vomit and the sweat of fear. People had been slammed about by the violence of the hurricane and their injuries added to the illusion of a watery corner of Hell. From below came the ominous slosh of water and the scout's pulse fell into synchronization with the *thud-weep, thud-*

weep of the pumps. Holten's friend sat on a bunk, bandaging the arm of a small girl, who cried hysterically while he worked.

"It's broken, I'm afraid. But there's nothing can be done for her now," Carlos told him with a sigh. "So many injured. They're all frightened."

"We threw cargo and those big, two-wheel carts over the side to lighten the ship," Eli replied.

"Hummm. *Señor* Mendoza will not be pleased."

"If he's a short, fat little feller in a fancy suit, he knows already and he's not at all happy about it. I had to rough him up a little to keep him from punching out the sailors who were dumping things overboard."

Carlos smiled. "That's him. All he thinks of is profits. He'll have had that cargo insured for double its worth, you can be sure."

"What can I do to help?"

A shrug and tilted head from Carlos. "Patch up those who are hurt. See to our horses. Whatever you can think of, *amigo*. The worst of it is over now, I think."

Nature made a liar of Carlos Ocampo as huge following seas began to crash over the stern rail and sweep across the quarter deck. Tons of frothing green saltwater poured below decks and the people screamed in fright once more. The vicious pitch and roll seemed to go on forever.

"I'd better check on the horses. They could easily fall and break a leg in this."

Two animals had already fallen in the special hold for livestock. Fortunately neither belonged to Eli or Carlos. Shattered bone poked yellow-white from the foreleg of a roan gelding, who screamed pitifully in fright and agony. Across the narrow aisle, a fat bullock had been slammed into the side of its stall with enough force to break the thick boards. One of the two-by-six planks had rammed its splintered end through the unfortunate animal's side and ripped into its vulnerable intestines. Steadying himself, Eli drew his Remington.

The roan showed the whites of its eyes and its head weaved like a snake's as the tossing ship fought through the waves. Holten took unsteady aim and drew back the hammer. His ears rang while brutal pain stabbed into his head when the firing pin landed on a primer and the .44 detonated. The slug slammed into the thick bulkhead two inches above the injured horse's right ear. Holten cocked his six-gun a second time and took a two-handed grip, steadying his aim.

Before he touched the trigger, the bullock on his left bellowed in pain and threw its weight against the front of the stall. A loud, sharp crack followed.

One heavy span of two-by-six flew outward and slammed into the scout's ribs. The impact drove him painfully back against an upright post. He nearly lost his grip on the Remington as it accidentally discharged. Fiery shafts of torment radiated outward from his savaged chest and involuntary tears blurred Eli's vision a moment. Gingerly he wiped them away with the back of his left forearm and renewed his grip on the revolver.

His third shot struck the center of the roan's forehead. The damaged horse stiffened and reared back slightly, then went slack. Death spasms rippled its body. Holten turned and faced the foaming mouthed terror of the ox.

Trailing shattered bits of bulkhead at the ends of his tethering ropes, the bullock had started forward out of the smashed gate of his stall. Holten retreated two hasty steps while he cocked the Remington. He brought it up as the broad shoulder of the powerful beast slammed into a six-by-six upright of solid oak.

A tearing sound came from the tortured wood, then a crack began to show as it bulged toward the scout. Splinters flew and the upper portion lashed out at Eli. New pain rioted in his shoulder as the jagged end of the post dragged over his buckskin shirt and tore into the flesh below. Stunned by the force of the blow, he reeled backward along the passageway, pursued by the wounded beast.

Another post arrested Eli's retreat as he rammed into it, sending new signals of misery up his spine. With a weakened right arm he raised the Remington and fired his fourth bullet.

Off center, the slug smacked into the thick bone ridge above the creature's left eye. The bullock bellowed and its forelegs collapsed. It swayed there a moment, then began to rise. Holten drew back the hammer on the last round in his six-gun. The menacing bullock tossed its head from side to side in an apparent effort to rid itself of the agony. Slowly it took another step.

Holten fired his final round.

The bullock stopped in mid-stride. Its head drooped and blood ran in a torrent from its mouth, dripping from its distended tongue, as it sank on all fours to a resting position. A dark, round hole in its forehead oozed blood. Lowing mournfully, it shuddered mightily and dropped on its side.

Eli watched it die. Gasping from his exertion and discomfort, he wiped sweat from his face and began to eject spent cartridges.

"I hope that's the worst I have to put up with," he

fervently declared aloud.

As though in answer to his petition, the rampaging wind cut off as though sliced away with a knife. The sea calmed and silence descended on the *Riena del Pacifico.*

Could it possibly be over? the scout asked hopefully.

Chapter 11

The respite lasted only a short while. The eye of the hurricane gave little time for the many tasks required to save the *Riena del Pacifico.*

Captain Garcia and his officers organized repair crews and set them to pounding timbers into place to strengthen the hull and shifts worked to exhaustion on the pumps, in an attempt to empty the bilges. As for the mizzenmast, nothing could be done about stepping a replacement in the short time, anticipated by the captain, before the back side of the cyclonic storm hit them. Eli Holten gave his efforts to removal of the dead animals.

"Save a haunch and we can have a hot meal before the storm comes," Captain Garcia called down to Eli as burly seamen hoisted the dead bullock onto the main deck.

The scout waved acknowledgement and stood aside while the ship's cook carved off a hind quarter and set to skinning it. A good thousand pounds or more less weight, Holten thought to himself as the carcass went over the side. And the horse would help, too. Noticeably now, the ship rode higher in the water. Fires were lighted in a special pit that could be emptied through the scuppers when the weather worsened once more. The cook's helpers prepared a spit and began to roast the meat, while their boss set a huge iron pot of cooked beans on a trestle over the blaze. In minutes, the sweet aroma of barbecuing meat teased everyone's nostrils. His task completed, Eli joined Carlos and the men shoring up the hull.

All together, the repair labors went on for an hour and a half. An unprecedented time, according to Captain Garcia, for the eye to hover over the serenely bobbing ship. Everyone had eaten their fill of the rotisserie-cooked meat, beans and tortillas, and the fire had been extinguished by the time the trailing portion of the hurricane struck the ship. Its ferocity seemed far worse, compared to the front, which had moved over them in less than two hours. Unimpeded by the greater resistance of mountains or even flat land, the whirling, battering tumult gained speed with each hour. It also increased in potency.

Separate waterspouts formed their deadly funnels along the leading edge of the hurricane's back portion. Tons of sea lifted high into the air, swaying and dipping, churned by forces that seemed to defy nature. In moments, the peaceful ship turned into a torture chamber for all aboard as it ran helplessly ahead of the murderous tempest.

Flotsam covered the sparkling waters of the Bay of La Paz. On shore, shattered palms, overturned and smashed palapas gave testimony to the horrors of the hurricane. Several thousand, not including refugees fleeing ahead of Iron Mike Madonna's free company, remained homeless. Battered and leaking, the pumps barely able to keep up with the rise of water in the holds, the *Riena del Pacifico* limped into port.

She creaked and groaned like some abandoned, delapidated barn. Four more persons, including two passengers, had lost their lives before the back side of the hurricane had passed over the ship and blitzed its way toward the mainland. The foremast had lost the top fifteen feet, carrying away the stormsail and snapped rigging littered the deck like so many large, lifeless brown snakes. Eli Holten had suffered two broken ribs when he valiantly dived overboard in an attempt to rescue two seamen trapped in the foul lines of the severed portion of the foremast.

He had saved one man's life and watched exhausted and helpless while the other sank beneath the punishing waves. His injury came when the crew hoisted him aboard in a boatswain's chair. The canvas sling, rigged with light lines, slammed into the hull of the *Queen of the Pacific* and Eli felt the two bones in his chest part with searing pain. His chest tightly taped, he walked down the gangplank alongside Carlos Ocampo when the ship tied up to a badly damaged pier.

"You are a hero once again, *amigo,*" Carlos told him. "You are to be commended by Captain Garcia before the military governor of Baja Sur."

"I don't deserve anything more than anyone else. We all had to do our best to survive the storm."

"Your modesty is your undoing, Eli," Carlos declared. "Think. You're a *gringo.* Your fellow countrymen are soundly hated by many in Mexico. They do not forget the war in forty-six. Yet you risked your life to save those of two common seamen. *Mexican* seamen. You've shown a side to *Norte Americanos* not seen before, nor even believed to exist, by most of my countrymen. They are grateful and they wish to make much of this discovery. So relax and go with the tide, *amigo.* We'll make arrangements for our horses, then take rooms at the *Posada La Merced* and await what will transpire."

"When can I speak to someone about Milo Madonna and Myron Henshaw?"

"All in due time. First let the officials make over you, then you can talk about unpleasant subjects."

Carlos hailed a burro-drawn taxi and gave instructions. A pair of small boys trotted behind, leading their mounts. As the pair rode through the city, Eli saw more evidence of the hurricane, also great turmoil, caused he soon discovered, by the invading army that threatened La Paz from less than fifty miles away. Refugees lined the streets, seeking shelter and food. Soldiers stood about, singly or in squads, uncertain what to do or how to help. Carlos waved a hand at all this.

"Don't be so anxious, *amigo.* What can your information do to relieve all of this?"

"Nothing, I suppose. But if I can convince the military to take decisive action, based on my knowledge of the people involved, then the pressure will be relieved and the usual agencies can deal with the hungry and homeless. You have to understand, Carlos, that these people, Henshaw and Constance, are essentially cowardly. They shy away from an excess of violence and personal danger." The scout went on, extemporaneously, laying out a convincing argument as he tried it out on his friend.

"What is needed is a reconnaissance in force, with enough troops fielded to cause some real damage to Madonna's army. That to be followed by taking all the available troops into the field and forcing battle at the most advantageous place. Get the mountains, or a river, at Madonna's back and overwhelm him with superior force."

Carlos sighed loudly. "*Ay de mí,* that's the trouble. There isn't a sufficient number of soldiers in the southern portion of the peninsula to do that. Nor is there a running river. You seem to have a sounder knowledge of tactics than any three generals in the Mexican Army. Even so, it will be to no avail, I'm afraid.

"Here the generals believe in superiority of numbers, even more than in arms. Vastly superior, as it is. I regret to say that it is needed. Why, some of their soldiers—Indians from the far mountains of the south—still believe it is the noise of the rifle that knocks a man down. The bullet can't be seen in flight, and so is superfluous to them. So, no general can trust odds of one to one or even two to one in their favor. If they cannot be assured of the ability to overwhelm the enemy, they will continue to do nothing and be destroyed piecemeal."

"You paint a grim picture, Carlos."

"One that is all too true, I promise you that."

Again, Carlos proved to be prophetic. After a showy ceremony, in which the scout received a medal for valor, and a lavish banquet, he asked for and received an appointment to talk with the military authorities. By then, a week after their arrival in La Paz, more refugees had entered the city. They brought word that Iron Mike Madonna's soldiers camped within an hour's ride of El Triunfo, the silver and gold mining town a scant seventeen miles from La Paz. Eli's appointment, however, turned out not to be with the generals, of which there seemed a superfluity, but with a staff colonel, who commanded, in name only, a depleted regiment of lancers.

"Come in, *Señor* Holten," Colonel Armando Hurtado greeted as an aide showed the scout into his office.

Hurtado had unexpectedly gray eyes and a fair complexion. Square-jawed and barrel-chested, he looked about to explode with inadequately contained energy. He showed Eli to a chair, poured them both tequila and returned to the leather upholstered, highback chair behind his desk. The colonel spread spatulate fingers and pressed them on the mirror surface of polished mahogany.

"Now then, *Señor* Holten, what is it you came to see me about?"

Eli hesitated, disappointed that he was not addressing the ranking officers in La Paz. "I had really expected to talk to General Alleman and his subordinate commanders about what I know of Milo Madonna and Myron Henshaw."

"Instead you got me." Hurtado shrugged. "I regret that you must go through this screening process, but since I was relegated to this desk, instead of being at the head of my *lanceros,* they have had to find something for me to do. Oh, it was not a demotion," Hurtado hastened to add as he correctly interpreted the expression on Eli's face. "My numbers grew too small. Lancers were detached for duty in Mulege, Loreto, Santo Domingo and El Medano to the north of us and at Todos Santos, Santiago, San Jose del Cabo and Cabo San Lucas in the south. Those latter, unfortunately, are lost to the army of brigands which now threatens us. That left me with less than a company to command. My superiors felt a colonel should have more responsibility than that and do a lot more to earn his pay. Now I am chief of staff for General

Alleman, shuffle papers and talk to people who think they have something important to say about the invaders. In your case, with the testimonial to your heroism and the bona fides of Major Ocampo, I would say that you are the first one of value I have encountered. Tell me about it."

"Myron Henshaw, and a woman named Constance Williams, were supposed to steal rifles, artillery pieces and ammunition for Milo Madonna. They chose Fort Rawlins, where I am a civilian contract scout, to acquire these items and other supplies." For the next ten minutes, Eli laid out all he knew of Henshaw, Constance, and Madonna. When he finished, he leaned back, accepted another tequila and sipped sparingly.

"None of the towns and villages so far attacked by this Madonna have had large garrisons," Hurtado informed Holten in a thoughtful tone. "They've been no test for a force the size of his. All the same, the attacks have been carried off brilliantly. Is this freebooter an accomplished and capable soldier then?"

"Yes, Colonel," Eli informed him reluctantly. "Before I left Fort Rawlins, my commander, General Corrington, provided me with a copy of Milo Madonna's service record. I regret to say that in addition to a natural flair for tactics, he is the product of American military training. He had been an officer in the Army of the Potomac during the Civil War. Reached the rank of colonel by age twenty-four. His particular accomplishment of note was an unusual employment of artillery and cavalry to create diversionary attacks that masked his true intentions. This unorthodox strategy saved many lives and brought him to the attention of his superiors.

"Madonna was considered a genius at tactics. Until,

that is, a young woman seduced him into blindness and stole vital plans. She was a Confederate spy. It destroyed Madonna. Not only his career, but his self-esteem. He left the United States, a defeated man. He deserted from the army and went to Central America. Unfortunately, he did not leave behind his ability as a field commander. I'm afraid he learned from the best . . . including Ulysses Grant, who is now our President."

Hurtado sighed heavily. "I shall make the general aware of these facts, *Señor* Holten. You have been most kind in bringing them to us. What can we do in return?"

"When your army goes into the field against Madonna, I want to go along."

"Most . . . unusual. But then, we are offering land and citizenship to anyone who joins the expeditionary force being organized on the mainland. I suppose General Alleman can attach you if he wishes."

"Thank you. When . . . ?"

"When can you see the general? I can't answer that." Hurtado rose and stepped to a large map of the Baja Peninsula that hung on one wall. He used the tip of his dress sabre as a pointer.

"Madonna's mercenary army has advanced up the peninsula with disturbing rapidity. He entered this spine of mountains before the hurricane struck. Fortunately for us, the storm delayed him a week. Reports now place him here . . . at a point only three or so leagues from El Triunfo. Once it falls, nothing stands in his way to La Paz."

"What about this expeditionary force on the mainland?"

Hurtado produced a fleeting, bitter smile. "They will be ready . . . some day. Officials on the mainland are jealous of their prerogatives. They are uniformly reluctant to weaken their own provinces by sending troops to Baja. It is a political thing, I assure you. The soldiers want to fight, are anxious to expel the foreign invaders. So are their officers. But . . . generals and governors of states are—how you say it?—dragging their heels at attempts to gather a sufficient force.

"Likewise, the people fear a large army. Too many of them remember well the French occupation. With the wrong man in charge, it might be decided to march on the capital. Such a force would meet no more resistance than Madonna does on the peninsula. An ambitious general could use that army to make himself absolute master in Ciudad Mexico and all of our country. So, I greatly fear we may see nothing outside of proclamations about this relief force."

"Politics and greed. They're the curse of every people, Colonel Hurtado."

"Too true. Even if this expedition got under way, I am convinced that Madonna would be in La Paz a week before anything effective could be accomplished. I believe what you said. Particularly that additional American arms were brought to Madonna by this Henshaw. We know of Madonna's raids in the countries to the south of us. That alone does not account for the size or strength of his present army. I will make this point most dramatically for General Alleman."

"Do your best for me, Colonel. If you sell this properly and let me talk to the general, maybe I can come up with something more that will insure a victory for your troops."

Eli and Hurtado shook hands. Holten left the meeting feeling dejected. He knew now that he had only Ocampo and Hurtado to back him. Eli respected Armando Hurtado for his frankness and his support. He didn't doubt the colonel's willingness to do something about the situation. Unfortunately, Hurtado hadn't enough rank to accomplish anything on a large enough scale. Ocampo could call upon a force of only seven *Federales* and, despite their eagerness, that still meant merely policemen. Alone, Eli realized, he could do nearly nothing.

And all the while, Iron Mike Madonna marched inexorably toward La Paz.

Chapter 12

Half a league east of El Triunfo, in a roughly circular box canyon, could be found the silver mine operated by Angel, Pablo and Roberto Morales. Also, they had erected there an edifice thoroughly scorned and roundly decried by the priests at the church in the small mining community.

The sweat lodge, built in the Yaqui beehive style of thatch, occupied a place of honor. The Morales family, and all those who worked for them, were descendants of Yaqui Indian slaves. Two centuries before, the Spanish had transported their ancestors to the area from their native habitat far to the north in the Sonoran-Baja desert. Rather than waste away as so many North American natives had under the onerous conditions of enslavement, the short, hardy, barrel-chested Yaquis thrived.

Those early Yaquis enjoyed sturdy, permanent dwellings, medical care and ample water, not only to drink, but to bathe in and wash clothing. They had eaten better than their usual tribal fare of scrawny desert rabbits, an occasional deer, lizards, ground squirrels, kangaroo rats and shellfish. With improved nutrition, bowed legs disappeared, complexions lightened and physiques grew and hardened under the enforced labor in the mines. While the local Indians in the same circumstances died in droves, the Yaquis bided their time, prospered, and ultimately found freedom and a chance to work for themselves when Mexico overthrew their colonial Spanish overlords and established an independent nation. Still, the Yaquis did not intermarry with their Mexican neighbors. As the years passed, they excelled at any enterprise in which they engaged. The Morales clan had been no exception.

Twenty years ago, the senior Morales, old *Jefe* Fortuno, had discovered a rich vein of silver. Chief Fortuno Morales settled down, proceeded with raising his family and began to gouge silver ore out of the mountain. Since then, the family had greatly prospered. When Carmella arrived, a week ahead of Milo Madonna's invaders, she spread the alarm.

Joy at her return was not diminished just because of an impending fight against yet another conqueror. Three goats, two pigs and a fatted calf were butchered and the *fiesta* lasted for four days and three nights. Angel, in charge of the mining operation, sent trusted men into town to purchase beer, tequila and other necessities for the feast. He was also to bring back information of the approach of any *gringo* army. What could be done about these foreigners had yet to be decided.

Dark and glowering, with heavy brows and a hooked scar at the corner of one eye, Angel Morales expressed his opinion simply and forcefully at a meeting of the miners and local farmers.

"We will fight them."

His younger brother, Pablo, rose, the heavy muscles of

his compact, five-foot-nine body rippling in the sunlight that filtered down through the leaves of a large *ciboa* tree. Pablo acted as overseer for the three Morales *ranchos* which provided food for the family and their workers.

"How can we do that? Carmella has told us they have cannons. Can we go against those with hoes, machetes and hands full of rocks?"

"We have rifles. The men who guard our mines have them also. Lupe Bargas there owns a shotgun, as do each of his sons. We are Yaqui! If we must make and use bows and arrows, war clubs and lances, we will fight!" Angel declared.

"And then what, brother?" the young, handsome dreamer, Roberto, inquired in a lazy voice, better suited to accompany his excellent guitar playing. "Do we go on to rid Baja California of the pestilential Mexicans?"

For a moment a bright fire glowed in Angel's eyes. Why not? The prospect appealed to him.

"Six generations of the Yaqui have labored in the mines," he declared passionately. "Only the last two have done so in what we mistakenly call freedom. Still, the *hidalgos,* the landed gentry among the Mexicans, look down on us. *Mierda!* Even the peons give us insults and less than grudging acceptance. 'To be a Yaqui is to be a warrior,' my grandfather taught me that. Yet, except to help free Mexico from Spain, and to join the Mexicans in the fight against Maximilian and the French, in the past fifty years, the hand of a Yaqui in Baja Sur has not known a weapon.

"Now, new conquerors come, *gringo ladrónes* who seek to rob us of our silver and gold, our land and our dignity. If we don't fight . . . if we lay down and play the good slave . . . then, my precious brothers and dear friends . . . then we shall most surely lose the freedom we so recently gained. We'll be less than men, less than dogs. And only the wind will be left to whisper about the mighty Yaqui, who defied the Spanish, and won the right to be our own masters from the Mexicans, only to lose it to a band of *gringo* brigands. No, my peace-loving Roberto, no! We will fight."

"Only to die like the rest who have resisted?" Roberto inquired, echoing the words of his sister.

Angel laughed uproariously. "Not at all, little Roberto. We'll be clever. We will withdraw and study and wait until the time is right. Then we'll strike a blow that will be heard over all of Baja California, over all of Mexico. To succeed where the Mexicans have failed will make our names live forever. Those who now scorn us will come on their knees to seek our favor. That way we will triumph over the Mexicans as well. To do that, we must first destroy the invaders. By our hands, the *gringos* will die!"

Iron Mike Madonna sat at the head of the table and poured wine from a dusty green bottle. The large feasting board had been erected under a spreading live oak, larger and more ancient than any building in the area. The free company leader had a special pack broken open and the fine linen tablecloth, napkins and solid silver service spread out. Along with these came carefully protected crystal wine goblets. It was a conceit he unabashedly acknowledged.

"Even in the midst of the madness of war, one can always be a gentleman," he had declared.

He ordered a banquet be prepared and invited his officers, and Constance Williams, to dine with him. He finished pouring and passing the wine, three empty bottles by his plate, and lifted his own in the classic pose of a toast.

"To the silver, gentlemen and lady. And to us."

"To us!" the salutation echoed around the table.

"We are less than twenty miles from El Triunfo. All resistance has crumbled before us. With the addition of *Don* Pedro Encino's bandits and ten other volunteers, our numbers lost in combat have been more than replenished. The time is ripe to launch a campaign that will overflow the pockets of every member of this free company beyond their wildest imaginings."

"Here, here," Ed Robbins seconded. "Tell us about the silver, Mike."

Madonna sipped deeply of his wine and licked his lips appreciatively. "The richest deposits of silver, gold and copper on the peninsula lie within twenty miles of us. Since the early days of the Spaniards, millions in gold and silver have been taken out of El Triunfo. So rich was the yield in the past that Oliver Cromwell, in his earlier days as a pirate and freebooter . . ." Madonna paused to let a ripple of chuckles make the rounds.

"Oliver Cromwell came to the Sea of Cortez to waylay the plate ships when they made passage from La Paz to the mainland. He and his English buccaneers stayed long enough that there are rumored to be a large number of blond, blue-eyed Mexicans in La Paz. Cromwell accumulated enough wealth to finance his murderous insurrection against the English King and make himself absolute dictator of England. With that kind of financing, we could take all of Mexico."

"It helped that Cromwell invented a fanatic religious cult to go along with the arms and armor he purchased,"

Myron Henshaw added in a dry rasp.

"Yes," Madonna accepted. "The 'Know Nothings' played their part, too. I believe you're a descendant of the last of his zealots, the Puritans, who landed in New England," the free company captain added maliciously.

Henshaw glowered and drank deeply of his wine. That his ancestors had come over on the Mayflower was a matter of enormous pride. That they, like the others, had been thrown out of every country in Europe for conspiring against the lawful governments of their hosts, was a fact they all tried hard to conceal.

"But the irony is that the loyalty of his soldiers, the mercenary dregs of the Continent and England, like the zeal of the Roundheads, was bought and paid for with gold and silver from El Triunfo, nearly half a world away."

"A point well made," Robbins, Madonna's second in command, conceded.

"Which leaves us with but two objectives to complete." Madonna ticked them off on thick, powerful fingers, used to gripping the hilt of a sabre or butt of a revolver. "The taking of El Triunfo . . . and the taking of La Paz. Once we have the port facilities and bay in our control, we can start mining operations over again and use Ballengier's ships to haul the ingots off."

"I've always been convinced that the smart thing to do is strip the country of all the riches we can get," Myron Henshaw countered, "in the shortest possible time, and then get away before we wind up fighting the entire Mexican army."

"There's no reason we could not," Iron Mike acknowledged cooly. "Assuming your opinion were valid. Even then, we would be able to hold on for a month or more. In that time a great deal of ore could be converted to ingots at El Triunfo and taken safely away by Ballengier. If actually pressed by the Mexican army, we can leave on the last convoy out. Precious metals can be sold anywhere. Once converted, accounts will be opened in the name of every man in the free company. We will all be rich, gentlemen, rich beyond counting."

A round of applause and a hearty cheer followed. During the ovation, Iron Mike bent to scratch Hannibal behind his big, alert ears. The mastiff whined and rumbled his pleasure deep in his throat. Madonna signaled for more wine.

While a local resident, pressed into this service, brought it, Iron Mike studied Henshaw with a jaundiced eye. It might be to his advantage, he considered, if this nay-sayer met with an accident. All in good time, however. First they had to take El Triunfo and then go on in triumph to take La Paz. Iron Mike smiled indulgently at his whimsical play on words.

Two more days had crawled fruitlessly by before an aide to Colonel Hurtado brought Eli Holten a summons to military headquarters. The scout arrived expectant, only to have his eagerness dampened.

"It is to talk, *Señor* Holten. Only to discuss the situation with General Alleman. I'm sorry. It's the best I could do."

They entered General Alleman's office together. With the District Commander was the military governor of Baja Sur, General Rudolfo Lopez-Portillo. After introductions and the ubiquitous ceremonial glasses of tequila, Eli went through his small store of knowledge regarding Captain Milo Madonna, Myron Henshaw and Constance Williams.

"Neither Henshaw nor Williams have been seen in the United States since the raid on the arsenal in Arizona Territory," Eli concluded. "It is my belief, based on this, and what I've previously told you about the pair, that they're with Madonna."

"Hummm. Most interesting. If they are, so then, by implication, are the weapons. Refugees have been questioned and some refer to a woman who wears a man's sarape and *charro* sombrero, leather pants and boots. She fights like a man and swears like one. Could this be your *Señorita* Williams?"

Eli thought of the soft, creamy texture of Connie's flesh as she writhed against him in the bed at the Eagle Pass Hotel. Cursing, fighting and wearing men's clothing? Part of him, the foolish part that still stung from the revelation that she had been an agent for Myron Henshaw, wanted to deny the possibility. From his last sight of her, smoking six-gun in hand, wearing riding trousers and high boots, reason dictated that it could be likely.

"I've never encountered her in such a fashion, but it's possible."

Armando Hurtado smiled behind his hand and General Alleman had a twinkle in his eyes when he addressed the scout. "You were at one time, er, enamored of the *Señorita?* Is that the case?"

"To my regret . . . yes," Eli allowed. *Damn!* Did it show that much?

"Of no matter here. Tell us how you see our current situation?"

"As you wish, General Alleman." Eli walked to the large map of the lower half of the Baja Peninsula. Small colored flags, attached to pins, had been stuck into the location of each captured town in the southernmost portion of the long finger of land. Others indicated the position of Mexican military units and a collection of blood-red ones revealed the present deployment of Milo Madonna's free company. Formed in a crescent, the lines of advancing invaders held the mountain town of El Triunfo at the center, between the in-curving horns. Holten sighed deeply, not at all pleased with the words he had for these men.

"Further delays can only result in the capitulation of one village or town after another. Piece-by-piece, Madonna has rolled up all isolated resistance to the south of El Triunfo. It has become vital that you meet him in force. Although the enemy is well armed and all are competent fighters, you outnumber him and can reasonably expect to resupply far easier than Madonna can. Now is the time to strike at him and strike hard."

"How would you propose to do this?" General Alleman asked with a trace of amusement.

"That's not for me to decide. But, if my opinion were asked, I would have to go with this: A frontal attack against his main force is essential. Meet the bulk of his army at a place of your choosing and bring him to battle. I would suggest a two prong strategy. While the army pins Madonna down in a pitched battle, a smaller force, comprised perhaps of fifty or so irregulars, should strike at his flanks and rear. Keep them confused, off balance.

Put Madonna on the defensive for once."

"Most . . . interesting," General Lopez-Portillo drawled. "You are a general officer in your army in *Los Estados Unidos?*"

"No. I am a civilian contract scout for the Twelfth U.S. Cavalry at Fort Rawlins, Dakota Territory. I'm sure you are familiar with that, Governor."

"Of course, of course. I was only curious as to your source of tactical knowledge."

Stung to the point of vanished diplomacy by the general's tactless remarks, Holten replied hotly, "More than twelve years of fighting Indians, General Lopez. I have had the honor of serving alongside a brilliant man, General Frank Corrington. What I know of tactics I have learned from him. In addition, doing battle with a crafty enemy like the Cheyenne or the Sioux gives one certain . . . ah, advantages."

"Well said, Eli," Colonel Hurtado remarked quietly, using the scout's given name for the first time.

General Alleman raised an eyebrow. "You approve, Colonel Hurtado?"

"Yes, sir. I have always maintained that we're risking total defeat by not sending a large force against this invader. It should be more than obvious, if I may have leave to point it out, General, that Madonna has more than enough artillery to level any *estancia,* village or town he comes in contact with, excepting possibly La Paz. Leaving a dozen or two dozen soldiers alone, under command of lieutenants or sergeants, to defend the walls of places in the path of Madonna's advance only drains us of manpower, while his men sharpen their skills at siege, assault and conquest."

"You speak hotly, Colonel," General Lopez-Portillo snapped. "Your words have a ring of conviction. Only, I wonder . . . ? Do they, and those of *Señor* Holten, have the virtue of accuracy? As you point out, small garrisons have fallen. The people, mostly peons and soft town dwellers, have been unable to aid our soldiers. The picture will look quite different when this mercenary captain and his army of rabble face us outside La Paz."

"I disagree," Eli inserted. "Madonna's men are hardly rabble. They are trained, experienced soldiers. By the time he reaches La Paz, he'll have every bandit and wastrel on the Peninsula joining him. He will also have an army flush with riches from the smelter and silver mines at El Triunfo. They'll fight like madmen to hold on to what they have stolen. You cannot afford to wait for that."

General Alleman sighed and raised a restraining hand. "What you say may well be the case, *Señor* Holten. Your contribution is invaluable to us so far. We'll consider the information you've offered and your views on tactics most seriously. The General Staff will be assembled then, and we will discuss our deliberations tomorrow. Thank you for your assistance."

Alleman's dismissal smarted more than the snide insults of Lopez-Portillo. His square jaw clamped in a hard, angry line, Eli Holten exited with Armando Hurtado. In the hall, the scout exploded.

"*Mañana.* Is it always to be tomorrow? *Hijo de la chingada!* I'm fed up with these stuffed-shirt generals and their *mañana.*"

"Son of a bitch," Hurtado repeated in English. "You swear most colorfully in Spanish, Eli. What do you propose to do . . . seeing you can't wait longer for *tomorrow?*"

"If I can't get the army off its collective ass, then I'll look elsewhere for someone to fight Madonna. Surely some of these refugees will want a swing at the bastard who ran them out of their homes."

Chapter 13

From the mountains in the southwest where the storms came from, ominous thunder rumbled as dawn broke over La Paz. The generals would not have to wait for their "tomorrow" to discuss the awesomely real danger of Iron Mike Madonna. The previous afternoon, following Eli Holten's revelations, Alleman had sent a platoon to reinforce the twenty-man garrison at El Triunfo. Alleman and Lopez-Portillo felt confident this would serve to handle the situation. The platoon's fate would soon tell them which plan had been conceived in wisdom.

Eli awakened to the familiar grumble of artillery. Blinking, he climbed from bed and padded to the pitcher and basin in one corner of the room. He washed his face and neck, then scraped off the overnight stubble from his cheeks. His gut tightened with each distant murmur. The battle for El Triunfo had begun, he knew. Dressed, his hair finger-combed into place, he went out on the street.

Breakfast first, the scout decided as he walked along *Avenida de los Heros Martires*. People stared questioningly at him. They instinctively distrusted his light skin and blond hair. Some spoke in hushed voices to each other, uncertain what the far off rumbles meant. Others knew, though, Eli observed. Their faces tight and eyes nervously darting toward the sound, they could only wait and worry. After he ate, Eli planned his day, he would go once more to Colonel Hurtado.

If he got no results, then he might make some efforts along the lines he described the previous afternoon. Somehow the idea of organizing a force of irregulars appealed to him. They could harass Madonna and delay him. With the fall of El Triunfo and the threat to La Paz imminent, perhaps the mainland generals would see things clearly and dispatch troops to push this Iron Mike Madonna into the sea. The scout entered a small restaurant and selected a table.

Holten consumed his morning meal without tasting it. His mind bubbled with ideas on organizing and operating a partisan force. Some he saved for later employment, others he rejected as impractical. By the time he mopped the last of the egg yolk from his plate with a rolled up corn tortilla, he had completely sold himself on the prospect. He went to the stable where Sonny was housed and saddled up.

For all of the apparent indifference of the generals, the military district headquarters bustled with fevered activity when Eli entered. The corporal outside Armando Hurtado's office informed him he would have to wait. While Eli passed time with a long, thin cigar, a steady stream of officers and non-coms, all carrying thick sheaves of papers, came and went from Armando's inner sanctum. A familiar and welcome voice interrupted Holten's dark thoughts.

"I see we both had the same idea," Carlos Ocampo boomed as he strode to where Eli sat.

"Carlos," the scout exclaimed in pleasure. "I'd

thought you'd been swallowed up in the social swirl. How are you?"

"Not any too happy right now. You heard the cannon fire?" At Eli's nod, he went on. "Damn the rigidity of these make-believe generals. If they would have put a force in the field yesterday, Madonna could have been forced to by-pass El Triunfo. We could have met them in the open and smashed his little army in less than a day."

"Five hundred men is hardly little, considering that less than three hundred are in or around La Paz to oppose him. It takes time to get the rest here. That's why I got so burned at them for delaying further. If Madonna came directly here from El Triunfo, he'd have the city in his palm before the first reinforcements could arrive from the north."

"I know it. I've come to the conclusion that if the army will do nothing, we will . . ." Carlos shrugged expansively, palms out and turned upward. "We will have to do it ourselves."

Warmed by this friendly confirmation of his own decision, Eli gave his friend the first sincere, well-intentioned smile in several days. "That's interesting. How would you go about it?"

Carlos wrinkled his brow a moment. "Circulate among the refugees. Talk with them. Surely more than one would be willing to fight."

"What about weapons?"

"There are some arms, confiscated by the *Federales* from criminals, bandits. Maybe fifty or so rifles, some revolvers. It might not be enough, but it's a start."

"We can attack at night, kill the artillery horses and pack animals. Make Madonna stretch his lines of supply."

"Yes, *amigo,*" Carlos returned, caught up in their spontaneous planning. "Ambushes in the mountains. Roll rocks down on their heads."

"Snipers to kill the men as they stand in line for the evening meal."

Carlos frowned. "Difficult shooting at best in the low light, Eli."

"You and I could handle that, Carlos."

Ocampo beamed. "We could. That's a fact."

"You two sound like you already have the battle won." Armando Hurtado stood over the seated pair, beaming with enthusiasm. He shook hands with both, gave them an *abarzo* and invited them into his office.

"The generals? Have they agreed to go along with what I laid out?" Eli asked at once.

"You mean, under the circumstances, eh?" Hurtado's brow wrinkled and his face darkened. "Unfortunately, no. They are still, ah, deliberating. Something has to be done, however. As it is, I like the sound of what you were planning. Anything that would delay Madonna's army." Hurtado paused and his lips formed a rueful grin. "Of course, at this stage, it would have to all be unofficial. You understand, no?"

"*Seguramente,*" Carlos assured Armando, with a broad wink, then repeated, "Certainly."

"Oh, of course," Eli Holten confirmed.

A large crowd of local residents and refugees had formed on the grassy quadrants of the plaza de armas, in front of the cathedral. Located on a high hill, overlooking the sparkling blue bay, ancient arbolas trees and stately palms shaded the area, where a fountain tinkled musically. A young woman stood in the bed of a high-sided, two-wheel cart. She held the frilly hem of her red-white-and-green skirt in one hand to keep it free from the dirty floorboards. Her other, she shook, fisted above her head. Eli Holten found the view oddly appealing.

"You know me. I am Carmella Morales," the girl shouted. "My brothers sent me here to see if there are any among you who still have their *cojones.* Your lives, your homes, your . . . everything is in danger. It is time to fight. For years you have sneered at us Yaquis. *Puro indio, los gentes impuro,* you say. Now the time comes when the 'impure' Yaquis lead the struggle against the *gringo* invaders, while you run about like frightened chickens in a henyard when there's a coyote around. *Basta!* I am disgusted. I am ashamed."

Eli admired the spitfire. She could hardly be more than five-foot-three, he estimated. Barely tall enough to see over the sides of the cart. Her black eyes flashed with an inner fire and glints of red showed in her raven tresses. Small, he reiterated, but nicely put together. The crowd shuffled in embarrassment and she spoke again.

"Well? You are still standing here. Where is the army? Where are those who would do battle to save their homes and their women? Or are you all women? *Sin valór, sin honór, sin huevos!*"

"Carlos," Eli began, "I think we ought to talk with her when she's finished."

"If she finishes, you mean. She's quite wound up."

On behalf of himself and Eli, Carlos invited Carmella to have coffee, once her harangue had ran its course. She asked scathingly if they, too, feared showing any resistance to the *gringo* enemy.

"That's what we want to talk about with you. I am the

Comandante of *Federales* in Mazatlan and this gentleman is a famous scout for the army of *los Estados Unidos*. We, like you, are interested in organizing some sort of resistance against *Capítan* Madonna."

The tiny Carmella favored them with a warm, beaming smile. "*Señores,* I am entirely at your disposal. Er . . . up to a point, that is."

They found a table at a sidewalk cafe. Eli ordered *cafe con leche* for them all and sweet rolls. Carlos urged Carmella to explain her involvement.

"I have seen what the *gringo* invaders can do. Murder and rape, the defilement of a priest." She stopped and cast a baleful eye at Eli. "You are a *gringo, verdad?* Why is it you are here and not with *them?* Are you a spy?"

"Oh, no, *Señorita* Morales," Carlos hastened to assure her. "He is a hero of Mexico, twice over. He killed two famous bandits who raided the train from Hermosillo to Mazatlan. Later he saved the life of a common seaman during the hurricane. He has been decorated by General Lopez-Portillo."

Carmella's eyes widened and her expression lost some of its hostility. "Still, he *is* a *gringo.* No matter for now. If he wants to fight, my brothers will let him."

"It is somewhat the other way around, *Señorita* Morales," Eli explained. "Carlos and I are organizing a resistance force to harass Madonna's supplies, his men and his freedom of movement. We thought that, from what you said, your brothers would be a valuable asset to our organization."

"*Sí,* it is as I said. If you want to fight on their side, my brothers will let you."

* * *

Nestled in a natural pass through the high, nearly treeless mountains that surrounded it, El Triunfo had existed for more than three hundred years. Along the narrow dirt road that led south to Cabo San Lucas, thick-walled adobe buildings formed the business district. To the east of this rustic highway lay the dwellings of the workers who labored in the mines and the smelter. To the west, huge smokestacks of native brick stabbed the sky, belching acrid fumes day and night. Giant crucibles of ore were heated in the smelter, the dross skimmed off and pure silver and gold poured into molds to form ingots. Black, arched openings dotted the hillsides beyond in all directions, out of which came a steady stream of men and ore cars. Since early Spanish colonial times, the people of El Triunfo had prospered and lived in peace.

Even the violent upheaval of the separation from Spain and the recent struggle to oust Maximilian had barely rippled this calm. Then came the human locust of Iron Mike Madonna's mercenary army. Because of the terrain and layout of the town, no wall had ever, nor likely could have been built around El Triunfo. As a result, Madonna ordered only a brief cannonading of the buildings.

"We have to properly impress the locals," Iron Mike explained when he checked the positioning of the artillery and ordered that ten rounds be fired from each piece, over a period of one hour.

For some reason, which Iron Mike could not understand, the natives had not been properly impressed. Although one smokestack had been holed in three places, a pile of brick rubble laying at its base, and a fire burned in the municipal government's block-square building, no sign of surrender had been shown.

"Ed, these people are more stubborn than I expected," Iron Mike admitted to his second in command at the end of the shelling. "Send in the cavalry. Have them ride through those houses over there. Most of them have thatched palm roofs. Set them on fire."

"What about the guns, Mike?"

"Put the light gallopers out on the flanks and have them lob a few shells into the town from time to time. Keep clear of where our men will be, but you have an area three blocks long by four deep to work on."

"Shouldn't we concentrate on the smelter?"

"No. We don't want to damage any more machinery. The place has to be operational for us within a few days. Lay your guns on those stores along the main road. Get the shelling started, then send in the cavalry. Oh, and have Henshaw and Connie report to me, will you?"

"Right," Ed Robbins acknowledged as he turned his mount's head and lightly flicked its flanks with the round knobs of his military spurs.

"Oh, Mike, it's going marvelously," Constance Williams burbled as she rode to Milo Madonna's side. "Why, they've not even fired a shot at us."

"We're out of rifle range, back here behind the cannon," Iron Mike reminded her.

"Oh. I never thought of that. Ah, what is it you wanted?"

"Let's wait until Henshaw gets here, shall we?"

"Do we have to?" Constance teased.

"I want him to fully understand what I have in mind. You see, Connie, I've been trying to come up with some means of utilizing your, ah, talents to the advantage of this campaign."

Connie brightened, her face animated by the emotions

within. "That's wonderful. I feel so . . . so useless just riding along, firing a revolver from time to time. I'll do anything you want. You'll be proud of me, too."

Madonna had to smile. "I'm sure I will."

"Myron doesn't own me, you know," Constance offered suggestively. "And . . . lately, I . . . well, I've come to see that there's a great deal of difference between Myron and . . . a man like you. I greatly admire . . . no, that's not the proper word. I'm strongly attracted to you, Mike. Lately I often lay awake at night wondering if that 'Iron Mike' applies to *all* of you."

Madonna felt a stirring in his loins. Despite the loveliness and obvious availability of Constance, he fought the impulse. It wouldn't do. Not now.

"A soldier who's drained of all his sap ain't worth a damn in a battle," U.S. Grant had once told him. Milo Madonna believed it.

Some other time, some other place, he'd jump her in an instant. Perhaps, he speculated, after the fighting ended. After he'd taken care of Henshaw. . . .

"What? I didn't hear what you said," Iron Mike struggled back into the conversation.

"I said we'd talk about that later. Here comes Myron."

"Good." Iron Mike raised himself in his stirrups and waved a salutation to Henshaw. "Myron, it looks like we're going to have an easy time of it. Come on over, I have something to tell you."

While Myron Henshaw walked his mount to where the man and woman waited, the cavalry broke from behind a screening hill and thundered down a long slope toward El Triunfo. Wild yells and the drumming of hoofs could be clearly heard on the low promontory where the three freebooters observed the opening of battle. Although he had summoned them for an important revelation, Iron Mike raised a hand to command silence while he watched intently.

Less than two hundred yards and the mounted troops would be in among the houses.

A curtain of gray-white smoke billowed from windows overlooking the slope.

All but two men in the first line of cavalry spilled from their saddles. The crackle of rifle fire reached the hill a moment after the first man spread his arms and flew from his horse's back. Iron Mike watched, open mouthed, while another writhing snake of powder smoke formed against the walls of the thatch-roofed houses.

"My God, so that's where they are," Myron Henshaw gasped in awe and surprise.

"We'd better hope that's the only place," Iron Mike amended.

"Why's that?"

"We're vulnerable on our flanks and to the rear, Myron," Madonna explained. "If they have men out there in the barrancas, they could raise a lot of hell before we could do anything about it. Now, I wanted to see you two about something important. Basically, I've come up with an idea of how Connie can do a lot to further the expedition."

"But the danger . . ." Henshaw started to protest.

"There's no danger in this. Listen first, then comment. La Paz is full of refugees, strangers. Another one wouldn't be particularly noteworthy. I've decided to send Connie in there to get details on any defense preparations, troop strength, what the civilians are doing. A complete report is what I want. If possible, I'd like some idea of the water supply, food sources and quantity, what the Church is doing. Some of these Papist priests have urged their flock to surrender to us. Others led the fighting. I want some idea as to what the clergy in La Paz intends to do. Can you get all that for me, Connie?"

"Not alone, she can't," Myron Henshaw interrupted. "You're asking too much."

"I'll answer for myself, Myron. Yes, Mike. I can do it. I'd be proud to help any way I can."

"No, Connie," Myron protested. "If you go, I'm going, too. A woman alone is vulnerable," he appealed to Iron Mike. "A man and, er, wife would attract considerably less attention. Travelers, stranded by the invasion. We could make that story believable."

"You've a good point, Myron," Iron Mike allowed. "All right. We'll do it that way. Make what preparations you need and be ready to pull out for La Paz within an hour."

An instant later, the boom of shotguns and crackle of rifles broke out on the left flank of the freebooter army. A second later, more shots sounded from behind the lines. Worry lines creased Iron Mike's brow as he heard what sounded a lot like Indian war cries.

Chapter 14

"I do not trust the *gringo,*" Carmella Morales spat while she walked beside Carlos among the refugee men who had queued up to volunteer to fight.

"*Mija,* he is what he says. Trust me in this," Carlos replied. "You are a forceful . . . no, a compelling speaker, a true patriot and a lovely young woman. Ah . . . not necessarily in that order."

"*Señor!*" Carmella declared in a mock-scandalized tone. "I think you are trying to romance me."

"Not at all. Or rather, that's not the foremost thing in my mind. Eli Holten is a man of honor, courage and dedication. You may trust him fully. The thing is, he blames himself for our current difficulties. When two persons escaped justice in his country he felt responsible. They are supposed to be with the mercenary army. Their job had been to bring weapons, which, evidently, they finally did. Eli intends now to finish what he started in his country nearly a year ago."

Carmella stopped walking. "These, ah, two persons. One of them is a woman, no?"

"Er, why do you say that, Carmella?"

"I know what I know," she answered enigmatically.

"You are *indio,*" Carlos accused, then softened it. "As I am."

"I am Yaqui. That makes the difference," Carmella teased. "You say that the *gringo* is a hero. That he saved lives here in Mexico and killed notorious bandits? Tell me more about this."

Carlos readily complied, giving exacting detail of the scout's exploits since arriving in Mexico. While he did, Eli worked across the square with a line of volunteers who had already signed up to fight. His primary concern was their weapons or lack of them.

"You do not have a rifle?" the scout inquired of the next man in line.

Clad in a straw sombrero, white cotton shirt worn outside trousers of the same material, bare feet in leather huaraches, the volunteer shrugged eloquently.

"How would I get one of these, *Señor?* I'm but a peon. It is not permitted."

"Well I'll be damned," Eli remarked to himself. Then he addressed the short farmer. "In my country there are no such restrictions. Maybe that's why we've never been successfully invaded. Over there, then, with those others. Next."

"*Llamado* José Ramon Descalso. I am a *caballero* and have both a rifle and a *pistola.* I have come to fight the invaders."

"*Con mucho gusto, Don* José," Eli responded. "You are welcome. Could it be that you might obtain more weapons for these men who have none?"

Descalso looked with disdain at the cluster of peasants. "*Peones* with rifles? *Madre de Dios!* They might kill us all. It is unheard of."

"Peasants and Indians defeated the French, did they

not?" Eli taunted. "These men are willing to fight the enemy. They deserve the best we can arrange."

Still not entirely convinced, Descalso shrugged. "I will talk with my *compañeros*. Those who must remain on the ranch can spare a few rifles."

"Good, good," Holten encouraged the man. "Everything helps. Now, who's next?"

Eli Holten and Carlos Ocampo sat at a table outside a popular cantina on the *melacón*. To the scout's left, the sun slowly sank toward the distant spine of mountain peaks that divided the Baja Peninsula. Gulls circled the bay, crying raucously as they sought a supper of anchovies and other small fish. Pelicans glided serenely through their noisy formations and plunged to fill distended beaks with water and wriggling food. Holten sipped from a concoction of rum and coconut milk. Both men rose as Carmella Morales approached, hips swaying in a tantalizing rhythm.

"I had hoped to find you here, Carlos, Eli."

Holten's right eyebrow rose quizzically at this use of his first name. Carmella flashed him a smile and accepted a chair. She nodded toward the drink in Eli's hand.

"Don't drink many of those, Eli, and expect to stand up suddenly," she teased. "I will have the same, please."

When she spoke to him, Carmella's tone was warm, honeyed. Her posture, gestures and expression promised things the scout would never have expected. He broke off from their locked gaze to signal the waiter.

"It is going well," Carmella continued. "We've more recruits than I ever expected."

"There'll be more tomorrow," Eli assured her. "Carlos

explained it to me. Those who signed up today will be celebrating and bragging tonight. Their friends will feel compelled to do so or look less than a man. It's a matter of *machismo.*"

"You are learning the character of Mexican men well, Eli," Carmella complimented him. "Though I suppose it is the same among the Yaqui. Not a one of our men at El Triunfo declined to join my brothers. Angel is leading, Pablo is his aide. Roberto is organizing weapons, ammunition, explosives."

"Explosives?" Carlos asked, surprised.

"*Sí.* Blasting powder from the mine. These *gringo ladrónes* will soon be sorry they ever came into our mountains."

"Ah . . . what about some supper?" Eli inquired.

Carlos had been studying the meaning-laden looks exchanged between Carmella and Eli. He saw the raw need of both as though inscribed on their foreheads and knew that they were only too aware of it also. He finished the last of his straight rum and pushed back from the table.

"Not for me, I'm afraid. I'm for an early bed. There's much to do tomorrow. Eli, what will you be teaching those who do not have firearms?"

"I have a few ideas. I'll work on them tonight and let you know in the morning."

"All right, then. Have a good rest and we'll start early. Say . . . six in the morning?"

"Sounds good to me." After Carlos departed and Carmella had taken a long sip of her drink, Eli leaned close. "Where is a good place to eat?"

Carmella pointed to the east, along the curve of the bay. "*El Pescador* is right there. They have wonderful food. Especially the shellfish. Oysters and clams make a man stay proud all night, you know."

"No," Eli answered soberly, his heart racing. "I didn't know that, but I'm willing to give it a try and find out."

"*Bueno.* You are refreshingly direct, like Yaqui men. The Mexicans I have known take so long to get around to making a, ah, point. We will eat, then we shall see if what is said is true."

Eli and Carmella drained their glasses and the scout paid the bill. Together they strolled along the *melacón* as the last lingering orange glow of the sunset faded from the bay, replaced by the soft light of kerosene street lamps. They neared the restaurant when Carmella spoke again.

"I thought all day about how to make up to you for my unkind thoughts and words. This is the best of all ways, is it not?"

"What brought all this on?"

"Carlos has told me about you and now I wish to be friends. You are tall, handsome, strong. A hero of Mexico. Could a woman ask for anything more?"

"Let's eat, then we can discuss that."

Carmella gave him a secret, knowing smile.

Eli Holten consumed a mound of raw oysters and clams, dipped in a fiery red sauce, then demolished a whole lobster, broiled over mesquite wood. All through the meal, Carmella's leg pressed tightly against his. On occasion, their fingers would touch and the scout felt an electric shock spread through his warming body. By the time they ambled to the *Posada la Merced,* the scout had an erection that pressed insistently and painfully against his trousers. Without discussion, they went to Holten's room and Eli led Carmella inside.

A moment after the door closed, Eli bent and lifted Carmella off the floor, then kissed her fervently on lush, ripe lips. Her agile body writhed against his and he released his hold with one hand to fumble at the ties of his beltless dress trousers.

Carmella relieved him of that duty when their kiss ended and he set to removing her blouse. The Yaqui girl shivered with delight as the scout's big, strong hands caressed the bare skin of her chest and back. She moaned with happiness as his thumbs began to grind against her nipples, making them rigid.

"*Ay! Tu eres un padrillo!*" she cried as she liberated his long, pulsing organ from its prison.

She encircled the rigid staff with both hands, small as a child's, and began to squeeze and stroke him. Eli gasped as she sent ripples of delight outward from the hairy nest in his groin. Then he asked her an earnest, though oddly timed, question.

"The word, *padrillo*. I'm not familiar with it."

"I say that you are a stallion. I have never seen such a magnificent *cholo* before."

Carmella bent and kissed the wetly-glistening tip, her tongue teasing its sensitive surface. Eli picked up her slight form with ease and walked to the bed. There he lay full length on his back and hoisted her astride of his bony hips. While he slowly lowered her childlike body toward the heated point of his fleshly lance, he raised his knees to provide her back support. Carmella eagerly reached out and guided his hugeness toward her.

"*Ay!*" she cried out as he pierced her wet, pink folds. "*Ayyyy! Ayyyy! Ayyyy!*"

A tightness, like none Eli had experienced since his first youthful encounter with a virgin, gripped his massive phallus as bit-by-bit it disappeared into the small passage that hotly welcomed it. For a moment he feared he might rip her apart. The wild light in her eyes soon told him that he need not worry. Passion and joy, not pain, brought the cries from her straining throat.

Head thrown back, Carmella shuddered with continual spasms of sheer delectability as Eli penetrated farther into her than any male had previously managed. Delirious sensation exploded through the scout's body as he began to thrust forward and back. Weight borne on his heels and shoulders, he drove his massive engine through a silken tunnel that contracted in madly satisfying ripples. Carmella arched her back and pressed against his knees while she strove to match his rhythm. Love's sweet sweat glistened on their bodies and Carmella began to keen out a continuous litany of delirious pleasure.

The wooden bed, with leather lacings, creaked and shrieked in time with their movements, matching the wails of utter bliss that came from the surging, pumping girl. Eli's heart pounded and his belly ached. His breath came in short, noisy gasps and vision blurred as starbursts of bright color expanded behind his eyes.

"*Ayudame! Ayudame!*" Carmella screamed as she dissolved into magnificent climax.

Holten could do much to help her and he went at it with a will, pumping harder so that she quickly raced up the slope once more. Shuddering throughout her whole length, Carmella exploded a third time before the scout felt his own precipitous dash toward the ultimate.

His burning wetness filled her as Eli whirled off into oblivion. Exhausted, thrilled beyond belief, Carmella fell forward onto the scout's body, her cheek resting on his chest. They lay for a long time, joined together by his still-rigid maleness. Carmella whimpered when at last Eli began to withdraw.

Once he had completely disengaged, Carmella raised herself and settled on all fours. "Quickly," she pleaded. "Before it goes away, mount me like the stallion you are. Hurry, *amado,* hurry. I ache for the need of you."

Excited anew and anxious to taste of Carmella's further delights, the scout positioned himself and slid his iron-hard length between her wide-spread thighs until its tingling tip glided between the portals of her pleasure purse. With fervent sincerity he hoped the legends about shellfish proved to be true.

Chapter 15

As expected, *Campo Militar Numero Cinco* proved to be deserted when the night time chorus of desert insects gave way to the sweet call of morning doves, imperious whistling of quail and the cheeky scolding of ground squirrels. The night chill still remained when a slightly sore and immensely pleased Eli Holten led the unarmed volunteers onto the abandoned military post. A bloated orange ball slowly made its daily appearance at their backs, turning the crystalline droplets of dew into a constellation of myriad, multi-colored diamonds. In silence, Holten directed his charges to the center of the empty strip of cactus-strewn land.

"Since you men have no guns, and we cannot provide enough for you, the solution is simple," the scout told them. "You will have to get them for yourselves. From the enemy. You all have knives, machetes, even hand sickles. Those of you who do not know how to effectively use them against humans will be taught. Those of you who do will be the teachers and become corporals in our little army of irregulars."

"*Señor,*" one young, stalwart peon inquired. "How is it we will go about getting firearms from the enemy?"

"You will work in pairs. Each two-man group will be

assigned to the task of slipping up on enemy sentries and killing them quietly. You will then relieve them of their rifles and other weapons and equip yourselves prior to any attack. If all goes right, you should be all well armed before the end of the week."

"*Madre de Dios!*" one recruit exclaimed.

"*Santa Maria y todos los Santos,*" another breathed out in awe.

"Can we really do this thing?" a short, stocky peon with the face of an angel and the physique of a blacksmith inquired.

"Yes. If you apply what you learn in the next day or so."

A rumble of cannon fire came through the early morning from the direction of El Triunfo. At least the small town still held out, Holten thought gratefully. Not without cause, the scout wondered what Iron Mike Madonna might have in mind for La Paz. He shoved the morbid reflection away and raised his voice so all could hear.

"I want all of those who know how to fight with a knife to raise your hands. This is not a time to concern yourself with whatever you might have been before today. Now you are soldiers of Mexico, fighting for your country."

He eyed the shifty-looking character to his right in the semi-circle who hesitantly raised his right hand. Two more did the same. Then a trio of strong, clear-eyed men who might have been cowboys also raised their arms.

"Good. Now, the rest of you break up into groups of five. Two of the instructors will work with each group."

With ominous persistence, the cannon continued to thunder.

* * *

Iron Mike had been right. So far, no one had questioned them in the least. Constance Williams pointed that out to Myron Henshaw in a quiet voice as they walked along the *prado* on the west side of the plaza de armas in La Paz.

"We've never once been asked for our papers or has anyone inquired about what we're doing," she bored in with determination.

"That's quite true, my dear. Bear in mind, though, that we've only been here for a matter of an hour or so."

Unimpressed by this, Constance went on. "We've seen plenty of soldiers, yet none of them appear to be preparing for any sort of troop movement. Except for these throngs of refugees and their restless moving around, the city seems to be peaceful enough. What we need is to talk to someone who knows what is going on."

"We can go to the ferry office. Pretend we're trying to flee the fighting by going to the mainland. Perhaps we can learn something that way."

"That's a good idea, Myron. I'm glad you came along," she added sweetly. Then her voice grew cold, hard. "What we really need to do is go down to a place where there are policemen and soldiers, looking for anything suspicious or out of the ordinary, and draw attention to ourselves. Hell, we don't even speak the language. What do you expect to find out that way?"

Myron Henshaw gritted his teeth. "That's enough, Constance. It *is* a good idea because it fits in with what we're trying to pass ourselves off as. We would be expected, as legitimate travelers, to try to find a way out of here."

Constance gave his remarks long, serious consideration. With her new-found self-confidence and the importance of the mission entrusted to her by Milo Madonna, she hated to admit he might be right. *Real* travelers, caught up in a foreign war, would make all sorts of noise, trying to get away. Maybe they should go to the ticket office. Before she could share this with Henshaw, movement on the opposite side of the plaza caught her attention.

A double file of men marched into the plaza area, over where a table had been erected for some sort of undiscovered activity. They were tired, sweaty, their clothing dust-streaked. Each appeared to be armed with some sort of knife or other edged weapon. Some of those mere farm implements. At the head of the double file walked a familiar figure, a face Constance knew she would never forget. She placed a hand on Myron's arm and nodded in the direction of the new arrivals.

"Eli Holten. I'm sure of it," she said breathlessly.

Not so familiar with the scout, Henshaw stared hard at the man obviously in charge of the others. "It can't be. What would he be doing here?"

"Looks like he's training troops," Constance returned. "I get the feeling that what we've been looking at over there is some sort of recruiting to get men to fight against Mike's army. We'd better get out of here before Eli recognizes us."

"*Destacamento . . . Alto!*" Eli Holten commanded.

Twenty-one men came to an abrupt, foot-stomping halt. Holten faced them to the left and paced before them. He looked the volunteers up and down a moment before casting a casual-seeming glance in the direction of Constance and Myron.

"We'll work on this again tomorrow. You did well. When we're through, you will be experts. You are dismissed until after the noon meal."

"What? No *siesta?*" one self-appointed humorist inquired.

"We're going to have to forget about *siesta* for some time to come," Eli answered him.

A chorus of groans followed his declaration as the men broke ranks and started off for where they could find something to eat. Eli began to walk purposefully toward where Constance and Myron stood. Immediately, Constance steered Myron away from the crowded plaza.

"Stop them," Holten shouted in Spanish. "Stop that man and woman."

Hampered by her skirt, Constance began to run.

Holten started after them. Henshaw spotted an alleyway that paralleled the cathedral and drew Constance into it with him. By the time Eli reached the mouth of the narrow passage, they had disappeared. He trotted on, hand on the butt of his Remington revolver, seeking some indication of where they had gone.

"Cuidado! Estupido gringos!" a man shouted from the next street.

Eli broke into a full run and came out on the next block. A vendor's pushcart had been overturned. Several varieties of fruit littered the ground and the scout had to dodge them as he hurried in pursuit of the dwindling figures of Constance Williams and Myron Henshaw.

At the next intersection, the two spies turned downhill, toward the bay, ran a couple of blocks, then popped into another alley. Holten got there in time to see a woman's foot disappearing upward over the parapet of a low, adobe building. He sprinted to the spot and gazed above. A tearing sound came from the roof. Holten clamored atop an empty barrel and jumped for the ledge.

His fingers closed over the lip of the parapet and he pulled himself upward by the strength of his arms. Carefully he swung a leg over and rolled onto the roof. Directly in front of his face lay the heavy traveling skirt and petticoats that had previously hampered Constance Williams. From a rooftop two doors away, Myron Henshaw took a shot at him that cracked past an inch above Eli's head.

Fisting his Remington, the scout returned fire at an awkward angle. His bullet screamed off red clay tile. As the morning on-shore breeze cleared the smoke away, he saw Henshaw and Constance start off at a stumbling gait. Holten came to one knee, braced his left forearm across the raised other and grasped his six-gun in a two-handed grip. He eared back the hammer with the web of his right hand and took aim. Gently he squeezed the trigger.

"Like yer sweetheart's tit," an old mountain man had told him as a boy. "Mild and steady gets it done."

Sound from the shot bounced harshly off the rooftop. Through the smoke haze, Holten saw Henshaw stumble as the bullet punched through the wildly flapping front panel of the outlaw's coat. It must have cut close enough to put a gouge in his side, the scout thought with satisfaction. He came to his feet and started after them.

Still hampered by her unsuitable footwear, Constance made slow progress. Eli began to close the distance between them. Myron Henshaw turned at the waist and triggered his Merwin and Hulbert in Eli Holten's direction.

The slug moaned off a tile chimney pot and sent a

shower of sharp-edged fragments into the scout's face. Blood ran from half a dozen shallow cuts. One made a steady scarlet stream from above his left eyebrow that obscured his vision. Holten brushed at it with the back of his left hand and raised his Remington.

Before the scout could discharge his weapon, Henshaw fired again.

An invisible sledgehammer seemed to lift Eli from his feet. Pain burned along the left side of his ribcage and he sensed at least one bone crack from the force of the bullet that had grazed him. He hit the slippery tiles heavily on the point of his right elbow and with his right shoulder. The Remington flew from his hand, to skidder some five feet ahead of him. Fine. Three broken ribs now, he mentally totalled. Through a haze of blood and misery, he saw Constance disappear over the lip of a roof three buildings away. Henshaw turned around to make his descent as Holten crawled toward his six-gun.

Before the fleeing spy started downward, he raised the Merwin and Hulbert for a final try at his pursuer. Tile chips filled the air a foot from Eli's body as the scout's hand closed over the butt of his revolver. Where the hell were the police? The army? No time to speculate on that, he told himself. Painfully he came to his feet and hurried onward.

When Eli reached the spot where the fleeing pair disappeared over the side he saw no trace of them. Excited chickens squawked in a backyard in the opposite direction. Holten turned and ran that way. He still saw nothing. Discouraged, he descended and set about seeking some lead.

Acting on the theory that if they headed toward the bay, they did so for a reason, Holten worked a zig-zag search pattern from street to street in the direction of the sparkling blue water. He continued for another fifteen minutes. By then, he had to admit his idea had proved fruitless. For all his effort, dispatching several policemen as well, he found no sign of the elusive pair. Once more Myron Henshaw and Constance Williams had escaped him.

The realization came with a bitter taste.

"General Alleman has to listen to me now, damnit!" Holten thundered in Armando Hurtado's office fifteen minutes later. "They were both right here in the city. Henshaw and Connie. Madonna had to have sent them as spies."

"Calm down, Eli," Colonel Hurtado urged. "You will see the general. I've already sent word that you have vital news for him. He'll see you in five minutes."

Lines of anxiety in the scout's face relaxed. "What made you do that, before I had even told you why I'd come?"

"You wouldn't shove your way in here as though the sky had fallen on La Paz for no reason at all. I assumed it was important."

Holten spared the Mexican officer a smile of gratitude. "You're a good friend, Armando."

When an orderly had ushered Eli and Armando into the general's office, the scout's urgency over-rode the amenities. Before General Alleman's aide could pour tequila, Eli revealed the presence of the spies. The news acted like an exploding roundshot.

"*Mierda!*" General Alleman shouted. He turned to his aide. "Alfonso, take my compliments to General Lopez and ask if he can come here at once. Also summon the other members of the staff."

"Sí, General."

"Now, tell me again about these people," Alleman requested as he walked to the small table set against a wood-paneled wall and poured tequila.

Eli reviewed his previous information on the outlaw pair and had only begun on the events of earlier when the other generals entered. They listened with growing trepidation and several muttered to each other, faces drawn into troubled expressions. When Holten finished, they erupted with questions.

The scout answered several, with what detail he could provide. By then his patience had been sorely tried. When one rotund, pop-eyed staff member posed another question, Eli passed his limit.

"Is there no way we can determine what these *gringos* learned by being here?"

"Yes, General Beltrón, there is. You get up off your fat asses, stop dithering like a roomful of old ladies and go out there and capture them. In the process, it wouldn't hurt to kick hell out of Iron Mike Madonna and his mercenaries."

"Here now," General Alleman declared.

"Condenación!" General Beltrón bellowed. "You have insulted me beyond forebearance, *Señor."*

Holten interrupted before the general could go on to the inevitable. "If you're going to demand a duel, General Beltrón, forget it. I'm not inclined to kill helpless people. I was about to suggest an alternative, when you interrupted me."

"Such as . . . ?" General Lopez-Portillo inquired, anxious to avoid any unpleasantness.

"A young woman from El Triunfo, *Señorita* Morales, has been urging refugee men to sign up to fight the invaders. Major Ocampo of the *Federales* and I have been helping her. We could take a lightly-outfitted unit in pursuit, observe what actions are taken by Madonna once his spies return, and report back to you."

The military governor's face brightened. He clasped a hand on Holten's shoulder and another on the arm of General Beltrón. "An admirable idea, *Señor* Holten. Yes. I can see considerable advantage in this. While you are on this mission, you can be devising a plan to mobilize our entire force and get it under way. Thank you for your generous offer of assistance. We will be in touch with you regarding its employment."

Holten started to leave when Beltrón yelled at him. "But I have not finished with this foreign upstart," he protested.

General Lopez-Portillo restrained his subordinate with a hand on each shoulder. He looked at the hot glow in Eli Holten's eyes, then gazed hard at Beltrón.

"Yes you have, Luis. Yes you have," he quietly told the enraged man.

Chapter 16

Massed together, the eight artillery pieces crashed in unison. The front of the municipal building in El Triunfo became shrouded in smoke, dust and flame. The two-story edifice shuddered and gave a groan, then a large section of the facing wall collapsed in a billowing heap of rubble in the street. Immediately, white flags began to wave in the smashed ends of hallways. Yellow torchlight illuminated the scene like a tableau out of the Inferno. A few shots sounded from here and there around town. A woman screamed. Then another. Amid the beginning sounds of their victory, Iron Mike Madonna rode down to accept the surrender.

"You fought bravely," Madonna told the three surviving soldiers and several smelter guards who occupied the structure. "For that, I spare your lives. Come down and stack your arms and you are free to go."

"What the hell," Myron Henshaw grumbled. "Kill them where they stand."

Henshaw brought the butt of his rifle to his shoulder. He'd not even aimed when Ed Robbins' big hand closed over the receiver and forced the weapon away from his body. Still smarting from their ignominious return from La Paz, Henshaw wanted to smash the steel buttplate into

Robbins' teeth. Sanity and reason counseled him not to do it.

"Where'd you think we'd be if we didn't respect someone else's flag of truce?" Robbins growled.

Iron Mike rode over to them. "You seem to forget, Myron. Those men will go away from here, spreading tales of our ferocity and the destruction we did. They'll also tell of our magnanimous clemency in letting them go unharmed. In effect, every one of them becomes an agent working for our benefit.

"If, on the other hand, you were allowed to gun down unarmed men with their hands in the air, the stories that would circulate would make others desperate enough to resist us to the death. How many times do I have to point out that we don't have an unlimited source of manpower? We cannot afford a direct frontal engagement with the Mexican military."

"Uh . . . you're, ah, right," Henshaw offered by way of grudging apology. "Where's Connie?"

"The last I saw of her, she was over in the burned out houses, helping tend to our wounded. I think her adventure in La Paz proved enough excitement for a while," he concluded in an amused, mocking tone.

"I'm sure it did," Henshaw replied, stinging from the implied criticism. He vividly recalled their breathless dash to escape pursuit, from La Paz almost to the outposts of the mercenary camp outside El Triunfo. . . .

"At first, I couldn't believe it," Constance had gasped out to Milo Madonna. "Eli Holten in La Paz. How? I had no idea. Sure enough, though, it was him."

"He recognized you?" Iron Mike had inquired.

"Yes. I'm sure of it. He knew Myron, too."

"Damn. Then he knows you were spying for me. He's bound to alert the military authorities. What did you find out before he saw you?"

"There's no sign of the army forming for any sort of campaign," Myron Henshaw injected. "Soldiers are standing idle around the streets. The people are all frightened. They're lined up to try to get away from La Paz by any ship or leaky boat they can get into. There's talk of food becoming scarce. Or at least that's what I think one of the vendors in the marketplace tried to tell us."

"Humm. A mistake not sending someone who could speak Spanish," Iron Mike allowed. "Go on."

"There isn't much more to tell," Henshaw had concluded.

"Tell Mike about the men Holten was drilling."

"What?"

"Nothing of real importance," Henshaw remarked casually. "They looked like peons. White pants and loose blouses, straw hats."

"He marched them into the plaza in military formation," Constance supplied. "They all carried knives of some sort."

"Very observant of you, Connie," Iron Mike commented pointedly, his hot, cruel eyes locked on Myron Henshaw.

Henshaw didn't like the implications that somehow he was to blame. . . .

He liked them even less now. He turned his horse's head away and gigged its flanks with spurs.

"I'll go find her. She has a good eye for jewelry and there's a lot to be evaluated in that silversmith's shop."

"Good. You do that, Myron."

* * *

"Eli Holten, these are my brothers; Angel, Pablo and Roberto Morales," Carmella introduced the three sturdy Yaqui men. She had brought them to the smokey, low-ceilinged, bayfront cantina where Holten and Carlos waited.

"The *caballero* is Major Carlos Ocampo of the *Federales.* This is Eli Holten, who is a *gringo,* but a good one."

Angel's expression said clearly that he didn't believe that one. Eli tried a smile.

It did nothing to soften the stern visages of the Brothers Morales. Holten cleared his throat and tried a new tack.

"I lived seven years with the Sioux. I am Indian by ritual, adoption, and by choice."

"We have similar terms for the same conditions in the language of the Yaqui. So you have relatives by ritual. Are we supposed to be impressed?" Angel demanded of the scout.

"No. I just wanted you to know that I will respect you, provided you respect me. That way we might be able to work together."

"See? It is as I say. They will fight for you, Angel," Carmella chirped.

"Not . . . exactly," Holten contradicted. Then he addressed Angel. "I gather from what Carmella said that you have a force of men already fighting in the mountains around El Triunfo?"

"We do."

"Fine. How large is it?"

"That is something I don't think we talk about now."

"Well then," Carlos injected. "Let's begin by showing trust in you. We have some two hundred men signed up.

Rarely does a larger force 'join' a smaller one. It's generally the other way around, eh?"

"That may be your way, Mexican," Angel spat.

"Have some tequila and let's talk about this more," Eli offered.

The three Morales brothers took chairs around the small circular table. Eli poured from a straw-covered clay bottle and cleared his throat.

"When I said, 'work together,' I meant exactly that. You know the area, we have mostly untrained men. Together we can hope for some sort of success. Alone, you are too few, and we are too ignorant of the mountains. Don't you see the obvious advantages of helping one another?"

Slowly, Angel began to smile. He extended a large, thick hand and grasped Eli's forearm in the Indian manner. "You have the smooth-working tongue of a medicine man. Yes. We can work together, Eli Holten."

"Good. Let's drink up, then. We have another man to see."

"When do I inspect your warriors?"

"In the morning."

"Time is short."

"So is life, Angel," the scout reminded him.

Colonel Armando Hurtado worked late at district headquarters. He, along with two sergeants and a trio of clerks, were the only occupants of the large, high-ceilinged building. Boot heels clattered on the highly polished tile floor of the long hall. The sound echoed off of large, stylized frescoes and ornate, baroque columns that formed arches to support the extended upper story.

Through the openings, Eli Holten and his companions could see the dark shapes of trees and flowering plants that crowded into the open, central courtyard of the Spanish colonial building. At the scout's direction, they entered Armando's office without knocking.

"Good news, Armando," Eli declared. "We've made contact with the leaders of the resistance around El Triunfo. May I present the Morales brothers—Angel, Pablo and Roberto."

"*Con mucho gusto.* This is a great step forward. How many men do you have?" Armando asked, picking out Angel as the obvious senior of the trio.

"Thirty-five men work on the Morales ranches and in the mine. All of them are in the struggle."

"Good. How many men have you and *Señorita* Morales recruited, Eli?"

"Right now two hundred and forty. More are joining us all the time."

"Hummm. I suppose, then, that you wouldn't mind 'finding' a caché of some fifty 'lost' rifles and two hundred rounds of ammunition for each, would you?"

"Hardly," the scout admitted.

"Another thing, before we get down to details. There's someone here I want you to meet."

A tall, painfully lean young man with pasted-down black hair combed straight back stepped forward from the window. He walked with the easy grace of a mountain cat. He wore a resplendent uniform of high black knee boots, white trousers and a green coat, heavy with gold braid. A wide red sash bound his middle. He bowed slightly, left hand on the hilt of a ceremonial sword, when the introductions were made.

"Captain Maldonado commands my remaining company of lancers, not on detached service. He and his forty *lanceros* are at your disposal."

Taken aback, Eli Holten stammered his reply. "Th-that's quite generous, Armando. Only . . . how? Won't General Alleman have some objection?"

Hurtado chuckled deep in his throat. "He has told me that the lancers will not be needed in the plans that are being drawn up. That they are to act as some sort of city guard." He extended his hands, palms up, and shrugged, a mischievous grin forming. "Is it my fault if I decide to send them to a different city than the one he intended? Surely, El Triunfo, which has fallen to the enemy, is in greater need of protection than this city that basks peacefully by the bay."

Holten laughed. "We have a term for people who use that sort of logic. In our army, they're called 'guardhouse lawyers.' With forty trained soldiers, we can whip these volunteers into shape enough to begin operations within two days."

Feeling considerable relief, Eli returned to his room at the *Posada la Merced.* The Inn of Mercy promised more than that tonight. Tiredness dragged at his body, yet he felt a heightened energy. Two more days and all this would be ended. The depressing thought did little to lessen the growing warmth that seeped outward from his loins. The flaccid sack of his maleness began to extend and enlarge. He inserted the key and turned it with mounting anticipation.

"You took long enough," Carmella Morales pouted.

She sat on the bed, wrapped in a gossamer robe that was so sheer her dark nipples tantalizingly showed through it. Holten crossed to her and hung his gunbelt on the bedpost. He knew the reason for her testiness. She had wanted to come along. The recruits had come as the result of her efforts. Carmella felt left out, ignored. He had no intention of pushing her aside because she was a woman, but her belief that this common custom was the cause showed clearly in her eyes.

"Your brothers used few words, though they talked a long time. Colonel Hurtado has given us the use of forty lancers."

Carmella clapped her hands in a girlish gesture of delight. "*Magnifico!* I . . . I understand that the Mexican officers would not have been pleased at my presence. They are . . . what they are. War is a *macho* game. I'm sorry I snapped at you. Perhaps, had I gone along, you would not have gotten the lancers. All is forgiven?"

Holten took her in his arms, brushed his lips over her cheeks, eyelids and brow. "There's nothing to forgive. Now . . . are you going to show me what you're wearing under that?"

Carmella broke away from his embrace and slid out of the wrapper. Beneath it, she wore only her lovely, tawny hide. Suddenly, Eli hurt with the surge of a full erection. It would be another marvelous night of uninhibited love, he rejoiced. Quickly he removed his clothing.

With fingers, toes and tongues, they conducted long, enthralling explorations of every contour of each other's body. They lay in a tangled heap on the rumpled bedding and probed into openings, caressed protrusions, nuzzled hollows. The banked fires of their passion grew to a conflagration and Carmella mewed like a sensuous kitten as the scout entered her.

Arms around each other, her legs locked around his

waist, they rocked their way gently toward an explosive communion that served solely to cause them to aspire to greater heights.

The heavens whirled during their second ecstatic coupling.

The earth shifted for the oblivious lovers at the ultimate peak of their third mad joining.

By the time their fourth frolic had become history, the cock crowed and pale dawn light entered through the high, narrow window of Eli's room.

Languorously, they began their fifth magic commingling.

Souls burned brightly as the heady titillation of worn, though finely tuned senses graced their amorous combat with frills of lace and vistas of paradise as their silken parts surged in perfect rhythm to a song they alone heard.

Hazily, they realized that the night had ended and day promised new dangers as they erupted into a geyser of mutual depletion and drifted off to momentary, blissful amnesia.

Chapter 17

Eleven men walked their horses into the narrow defile while mountain quail called cheerily and yellow-throated linnets made shrill interrogations of the mist-smudged morning air. All but four of the riders suffered enormous hangovers. Wrapped in vast confidence, following their defeat of El Triunfo and the fantastic quantity of booty taken, they gave scant attention to the terrain through which they ambled so lackadaisically.

Their incautious behavior was soon to prove disastrous.

"What did we get put clear out here for?" one member of the patrol asked in irritation as he rolled a cigarette.

"Iron Mike thinks there still might be partisans, lurking in the hills to snipe at our column," a British voice answered him.

"Shee-it! Them greasers ran like rabbits when we made the final assault on El Triunfo," the first man declared in a thick Southern accent. "They's all alike. No guts. Man, I could sure use a drink. I feel like someone split my head with an axe."

Three minutes later, someone did.

Red-brown like the soil, naked except for loincloths, a

dozen silent figures rose around the invaders as though out of the ground. Stout and stocky, the Yaqui warriors swarmed over the unsuspecting freebooters. Knives, hatchets, hand sickles and crudely fashioned spears flashed in the morning sun. Rising and falling, the blades soon became coated with thick layers of blood. The four sober mercenaries reacted quickly enough to draw their weapons.

None of them used their arms, though, as arrows whirred out of the underbrush and smacked meatily into their chests and stomachs. Two of the enemy groaned mightily at the immense pain that exploded inside them. Another made not a sound as he slid from his saddle. The fourth shrieked in agony and arched his back.

His motion caused the steel arrow point to slice open his aorta and his chest rapidly filled with blood. He grew silent as he reeled atop his mount and fell sideways into a large cactus. Eyes glazing in a prelude to death, the extra torment had no effect on him. In thirty seconds, the fighting ended.

Elated, Angel and the partisans melted away into the rocks. They took with them eleven horses, twenty-three firearms and an assortment of knives and ammunition.

Ten pack mules had been loaded with provisions for the advance detachment, which would pull out in the morning. The men who secured the heavy bundles stopped at noon to eat. Fifteen pair of obsidian eyes, and one of slate gray, watched them as they stood in line for their food. They had not even placed a sentry by the outfitted animals.

Their confidence in their safety was touching, Eli

Holten thought as he gave the signal to attack.

Two of the freebooters saw the shitless peons running toward them. *"Saõ Paulo,"* one gasped in Portuguese as he crossed himself.

Before he could raise an alarm or go for his sidearm, two arrows appeared to instantly grow from his chest and throat. Gagging on the obstruction and a gusher of his blood, he staggered about in circles until he struck a tree and fell over backward. His companion cursed hotly and brought up his rifle.

The shot sounded flat and far too noisy as he discharged his .45-70 in a spurt of flame and smoke. One of the peons clutched at his chest and fell to his knees. Another threw his handaxe like a tomahawk.

It split the breastbone of the mercenary who had fired his rifle. A fraction of a second later, a thunderous volley bellowed from the weapons of the attackers. Eyes wide with horror, the freebooter with the axe in his chest clutched at the blood-slicked handle while he watched his comrades die.

Five men dropped like bags of dirty laundry as the hapless invader's vision grew dim and his knees sagged. He managed to pull the hatchet free, which released a torrent of crimson. He uttered a soft, resigned sigh and crumpled to the ground.

"Get the mules," Eli Holten commanded.

Smoking six-gun in hand, the scout advanced on the remaining members of the free company detail. Three tried to flee. Of those, Holten took careful aim and shot one between the shoulder blades. Already dead, the man flung his arms wide and managed four undirected steps forward before he spun to his right and flopped over a large boulder. Another screamed in terror as a painted

Yaqui warrior rose before him and drove the long, sharp point of a spear through the mercenary's belly.

Angled upward, the lance tip cleaved through his diaphragm and halved his heart, before it angled to the rear and exited beside his spine. The third plunderer made it across fifty yards of cactus-littered ground toward El Triunfo.

There he stopped as though driven into a solid wall. Bullets smashed into his body from three sides. Held erect by frozen muscles, he swayed a moment, then he teetered over a dropoff and fell out of sight.

Holten rushed up to where four of his irregulars had rigged a dead line and waited beside the pack animals. "Get those mules moving. Head for our camp. We'll set fire to the rest of these supplies and join you down the trail."

"What the hell is going on!" Iron Mike Madonna shouted at his gathered officers. "What're you doing about it?" He slammed his fist against the plastered adobe wall of an intact building in El Triunfo and glared hotly at the men.

"I'll tell you what's going on. We're being attacked by fucking partisans. And you're not doing a goddamned thing about it, except for losing more men every day and night. We're in trouble. I mean to tell you we're in a worse situation than any since the campaign began." He stopped his harangue a moment, then pointed a trembling finger at Myron Henshaw.

"You saw peons being trained at La Paz and didn't attach much importance to it. Now you see the goddamned results. I want a large patrol, say thirty-five men, organized and sent out to locate these vermin. They are to exterminate the partisans to the last man. And I want you to ride along with them, Henshaw."

"Me? Whatever for?"

"You were supposed to make intelligent evaluation of what was going on in La Paz. Instead you get run out of town by a man who should be two thousand miles away from here. So I want you to see to it that this fucking army scout, Holten, is eliminated. Take charge of this patrol and don't come back until you can report that all resistance is ended."

"It is as you said would happen, *Jefe,*" young Manuel Garza told Eli Holten two days later.

Holten sat taking his ease before the evening meal in the camp established for his irregular troops some twenty miles west of El Triunfo, deep in the steep, desert canyons of the central mountain range. The delicious odor of roasting pork came from a huge copper cauldron, where *carnitas* were being prepared to feed the three hundred men under joint command of Eli Holten and Carlos Ocampo.

Long, slanted orange rays colored Eli's face as he questioned the apprentice scout. "Where are they, Manuel?"

"About three leagues to the east of here, only far to the north." He could not refrain from laughing at the image the searching *gringos* made in his mind. "They dash about with great purpose, looking under every rock for us."

"What direction are they headed?"

"North and east. Though some of them ride in circles

that go nowhere."

"Did you follow their back-trail to determine if this is the only patrol out?"

"*Sí, Jefe*. They are alone."

"How far north?"

"Maybe eight or nine leagues."

"How are they armed?"

Manuel shrugged. "Rifles, *pistolas*. Nothing more."

"No artillery?"

"Not even a wagon for food."

"You did a good job, Manuel. Ask Captain Maldonado to come over here, please."

Holten had the tequila poured before the lanky lancer officer had crossed half of the clearing. Geraldo Maldonado saluted rather stiffly, resentment for the *gringo's* command position clear in the hard lines of his face.

"Sit down, Geraldo," Eli invited. "Have a drink. I have something for you that I think you'll like."

"What is that, Colonel?"

"First off, I'm Eli to all of the officers. I'm not a colonel . . . in my army or in yours. Now then, a large reconnaissance force has been spotted by my scouts. Manuel Garza has reported on their movements. They are some dozen leagues from us, moving in the wrong direction. There are thirty-five of them. They have no artillery, reserve food or water and no provisions for their horses.

"Four hours before sunrise I want you to take your lancers out with Manuel and Rogelio as guides. They will put you into contact with the enemy.

"I will have left at midnight, with seventy-five irregulars. We will engage in harassment activities and sniping until you arrive. At that point, you will have the honor of leading your lancers in the total devastation of the enemy patrol."

For the first time since his superior, Colonel Hurtado, had assigned him to work subordinate to this *gringo,* Geraldo Maldonado smiled. He motioned to an orderly for more tequila and extended a hand toward the scout.

"Thank you, Colonel, er, Eli. The pleasure will be entirely mine. I've been thirsting to strike at these *cabrónes* who have invaded my country. You have given us the ideal chance to wet our lances, Eli. It is a chance to gain much honor. For that, I offer you my apologies and my hand in friendship."

"Done, Geraldo. Be sure your men have plenty of ammunition for a protracted fight. These mercenaries may be too stupid to know about lances. They might dig in and try to outshoot us."

A tight little smile made a slash of Maldonado's mouth. "If they do, they will regret that. There's little forage and no water to be had in that country. Some way, we will force them into the open and finish the *gringo bastardos* with our lances."

"*Buena suerte,* Captain. And . . . would you dine with me tonight?" Holten thought the Michohuacan style pork and roasted quail would appeal to Maldonado.

"On *carnitas* and broiled *cordoniz?* That's a sumptuous feast only a fool would turn down. Thank you, Eli. Again I am in your debt."

"You can discharge that debt by wiping out this patrol without any losses."

"I can but try."

* * *

"Estamos listo." The whispered message went around the encircling irregulars until it reached Eli Holten.

Everyone was ready. Perfect. There still remained a good half hour before sunrise. Within that time, the scout knew confidently, his silently moving irregulars would have killed all of the sentries put out to guard the encampment of mercenaries. When it became light enough to see targets, the snipers would open up. Thirty of his men waited behind an intervening rise to charge in the wake of the lancers.

Holten figured his partisans would have about forty-five minutes of sniping before the lancers, in their colorful uniforms, galloped down on the trapped invaders. In the event Iron Mike's troops tried to organize an attack against the snipers, the hidden riders would charge in to break up the resistance. It all looked good in theory. How well it would go, the scout could only contemplate and worry about.

"Send the men down to kill the guards," Holten instructed José Ramon Descalso in a low tone.

Within seconds, a dozen picked men slid through the rocks. With each stealthy step, they prayed they avoided any encounter with the many rattlesnakes who inhabited these mountains and hunted at night. In pairs, they set out to locate the six sentries targeted for death. Not satisfied to wait for results, Eli Holten left his command post and glided after them into the waning night.

Five minutes later, he came upon the first grim evidence of his partisans' success. The mercenary guard had been decapitated and his head set back on the ragged stump, looking behind him. That would give his relief a stir, Eli thought, when he came upon it at dawn. Silently, on moccasin-clad feet, the scout moved off in search of more victims.

The third supposed corpse he encountered reared upward from the ground, a broad-bladed ancestor of Colonel Bowie's iron mistress held sideways, tip up, sweeping toward Eli's belly. The scout felt a slight pressure against the front of his buckskin shirt as he moved sideways to evade the deadly thrust. Holten lashed out with the barrel of his Remington and made noisy contact with the wounded mercenary's head.

The adventurer grunted and tried to shake off the effects of the blow while he backhanded the Bowie and sliced through the armpit of Holten's shirt. By then, Eli had drawn his own knife and sent the tip forward, blade flat and glinting starlight from its upper surface as it drove between two ribs and pierced the invader's heart. Holten stepped away, panting.

Three more to check out.

Chapter 18

A thin line of pink-tinged white sky backlit the black, sawtooth silhouette of the mountains to the east. Eli Holten had at least satisfied himself that all of the sentries had been eliminated. A momentary surge of pride filled him when he considered that his green, untested recruits had done this without any warning being given to the sleeping patrol of Madonna's men. Camped in a shallow bowl at the northern end of the narrow canyon they had followed all of the previous day, the freebooters felt smugly secure.

After all, didn't they control everything from the eastern foothills south to the tip of the peninsula? In three days of sweeping the country they had located only two old, gray-bearded goatherders and their scraggly flocks. One of those had a boy of about ten along. He had thrown a rock at the searchers as they rode up, scaring the goats. If that could be considered a hostile act, they had seen all the partisans there were to see. At least, that's how Myron Henshaw figured it.

Restless, he had awakened early and made coffee. He sat sipping from a tin cup, wincing at the heat its rim transferred to his lips. Only the crackling of the fire and the dawn sounds relieved the silence around him. Was it *too* silent? Of a sudden, the question bothered him. He rose and crossed to where burly Sergeant Mehan lay in his blanket.

"We'd better relieve the sentries. It sounds a bit too quiet out there. Maybe a couple of them have fallen asleep."

"They have and I'll bust their asses," Mehan growled as he came out of slumber and threw aside his covering. Then he bellowed orders in his best NCO voice. "Perkel, Adams, Brown, Snow, roll out and relieve the guard posts!"

"Only four?" Henshaw inquired.

"In daylight, that's all we need. We won't be here more'n an hour, Mister Henshaw."

"The scouts?"

"Went out at four, like you said. We should be hearin' from them soon."

"Good. Get everyone up and start some breakfast. Somehow, I feel . . . trapped in here."

A strangled cry came from the direction of one of the guard positions. "Oh, Jesus! Oh, shit!"

Gordon Perkel ran back into camp, his face pale as last night's ashes. His eyes bugged and he worked his mouth soundlessly. He pointed a trembling hand, gulped and the words came in a jumbled rush.

"Weldon's-got-his-throat-cut. Oh, shit! I-went-out-there-and-he-was-lookin'-at-me-backward. Only . . . his . . . body . . . was turned . . . the . . . other way."

"What?" Mehan demanded.

"Somebody-chopped-his-head-off-an' . . . turned . . .

it-around," Perkel babbled.

"Post number four," a mercenary with more formal military experience than Perkel called out. "We've got a dead man here."

"Another one over here," Thad Brown shouted.

"Here, too," Bob Snow called. "God, it's cut awful!"

Worried voices mixed with angry ones and the surviving members of the patrol clustered around Henshaw and Mehan by the fire. One man's eyes suddenly bulged unnaturally an instant before his face exploded outward in a shower of blood. A fraction of a second later, the shouting men heard the crack of a rifle.

"Sniper!" Mehan yelled over the tumult.

Freebooters scattered in every direction, most diving for imagined safety on the ground. Plumes of dust erupted as bullets struck the hard desert soil and sent sprays of sharp sand and pebbles flying. Close to Henshaw, a soldier's body bounced up off the dirt and flopped back. He groaned and then began screaming as he touched his throat and his fingers came away smeared with red.

The bullets seemed to come from everywhere. Mehan crawled to where Henshaw lay behind a stack of mess gear. He waved an arm vaguely in the direction of the deadly fire.

"We gotta do something."

"Yeah. Those men over there," Henshaw remarked, thinking aloud. "They're closest to the horses. Get them mounted and send them after the snipers."

"Right. Only way. We're gonna lose some more, though." Mehan half raised himself and called out to the mercenaries on the far side of the clearing. "O'Toole, deVargas, Bouvier, move it out. Get to the horses. Start saddlin' ten of them. You other men over there, when they're done, join 'em. Go get those sons of bitches!"

So far his game of harassment and terror had gone well, Holten told himself as he examined the invaders' camp through field glasses. The snipers had held men in place, while the effect on morale of the gruesomely dead sentries had inhibited immediate return fire. The scout reckoned he had thirty to forty-five minutes left to hold out before the lancers arrived. At the present rate of development, it would do. Sudden movement changed Eli's mind.

Four horsemen raced from concealment within a thicket of scrubby live oak, quickly followed by six more. Bent low to their horses' necks, they spurred their mounts continuously as they streaked toward the positions held by three of the snipers. Crossfire tracked them and spurts of dust rose around their galloping animals. One man arched his back and sailed from the saddle. The others pressed on.

"Best we give them a bit more to worry about," Eli remarked to José Descalso.

Together they slid down the reverse slope of the hill from where Holten had observed the opening moves. Each hurried to his horse and mounted. Eli took the lead, mounted on Sonny, until they joined the waiting irregulars. Holten called them together and quickly explained the situation.

"We're going to have to charge the camp. Ten riders broke out to go after our snipers. The idea is to create a diversion, but also do all the damage we can. Mount up. We haven't any time to lose."

Over the sound of gunfire, Myron Henshaw heard the heavy drumming of many hoofs. Momentary elation filled him. A relief column. Madonna must have sent out another patrol. Then the riders came into view.

Most wore the white cotton trousers and pull-over shirts of peons, their straw sombreros bouncing at their backs, held on by leather chin straps. Most carried rifles in the haphazard manner he had come to identify with bandits. Only these men rode in military formation. Some wielded machetes like cavalrymen would sabres. At the center of the crescent file, Henshaw saw a broad-chested man in *charro* costume. He also recognized the large, powerful figure of Eli Holten, who rode next to the Mexican cowboy.

Damn! Pin us down, then sweep in to wipe everyone out, Henshaw bitterly evaluated. Holten had learned his lessons too well, working for the army. Well, Henshaw conceded, it looked like he had found the partisans.

Or rather, *they* had found him.

Swiftly, the charging irregulars closed to within fifty yards of the camp. Eli Holten rose in the stirrups and waved an arm over his head.

"Open fire!"

Along the curved double line of thirty-five riders, rifles began a steady crackle. Braver mercenaries rose before the onslaught, flame lancing from the muzzles of their weapons. Some stood their ground, while others turned to run for cover. Bullets bit into flesh and smashed gunstocks among the retreating invaders. Men fell, writhing and screaming in pain. Still the awesome cavalry charge came on.

"Pull back! Pull back!" a burly man with the red armband of an NCO shouted from the center of camp. "Fall in on a line centered on me."

Carefully Eli Holten gauged the rocking rhythm of his powerful Morgan stallion. He let his body and the Winchester at his shoulder find a normal movement, then sighted on the standing non-com. As his muzzle rose, Eli squeezed the trigger.

Sergeant Mehan, late of Madonna's Free Company, spun on one heel when the big .44 slug smashed through his heart and splattered out his back. Rocked sideways, he tottered a moment, then crashed onto the hard ground. More men died around him with each passing second. With wild, shrill yells, the improvised army of peons swarmed into the camp, discharging their weapons at anything that moved or stood still.

One mercenary, who had all of this sort of battle he wanted, leaped to his feet and attempted to surrender. A machete rose and fell, making a wet, meaty sound as it bit into his shoulder at the base of the neck. Blood spurted as the *machetero* swung his deadly blade once more.

Like a mishandled ball in some grisly game, the invader's head leaped through space and smacked solidly into Myron Henshaw's back. Henshaw howled in surprise and half-turned. In that moment, Eli Holten recognized him and urged Sonny in the outlaw's direction.

"Henshaw!" the scout shouted. "Give it up now and

you'll have a chance to live."

"Fuck you, Holten!" came the defiant reply.

Eli urged his horse closer. Henshaw raised his rifle and took a panicky shot. He cycled the lever action and pulled the trigger again. The hammer fell on an empty chamber. Desperately, Henshaw threw the Winchester down and went for his revolver.

His Merwin and Hulbert cleared leather and the hammer clicked into the full-cock position before Eli shot him in the right shoulder. The .44 six-gun went flying and Henshaw bolted to one side, face contorted with pain as he ran from the conflict. Instantly, Holten gigged Sonny and plunged after the man he sought to bring to a reckoning.

Henshaw made it to the unsure safety of a stack of saddles. There he turned, crouched and fished a two-barrel Remington .41 derringer from his left coat pocket. Around him he could see the discipline of Iron Mike's mercenary soldiers swinging the tide of the conflict. Many of the peons fought defensively now, backing their mounts from determined attacks by the howling, more berserk freebooters. Not so Eli Holten, Henshaw discovered a moment later as the scout's Morgan stallion crowded out the outlaw's view of battle with its broad, sweaty chest.

Reflexively, Henshaw yanked his diminutive handgun upward and jerked on the stiff, spur trigger. The little rimfire derringer made a flat report and smoke billowed.

Holten felt the sting and burning impact as the .41 slug cut a path across his right shoulder. He winced and hesitated a moment before bringing his rifle on line.

Henshaw fired again, his second and last bullet spit from the stubby barrel and cut a semi-circular notch in

Sonny's left ear. Despite the animal's excellent training as a warhorse, Sonny shied and reared in the air. It took all of the scout's agility to retain his seat as the stallion clawed for the sky. Then Sonny started downward.

Iron-shod hoofs lashed out instinctively as the Morgan hurtled toward the ground. When they made contact with Myron Henshaw's skull, it popped with a sound and a spray of red wetness like that of a burst watermelon. Sonny rose again and struck with both forefeet in Henshaw's chest, crushing his ribs and driving the splintered ends into lungs and heart. Holten exerted strong pressure on the reins in order to stop Sonny from further, unnecessary destruction, then turned his frothing-mouthed mount away.

Instantly he saw the optimum time for withdrawal had come and gone. He would lose men on the way out. For a moment he cursed his single-minded pursuit of Henshaw, then his eyes picked out the shattered corpse of the man he had come to Baja California to punish. An involuntary shudder rippled through the scout and he raised his arm.

"Assemble on me! Assemble."

Rapidly the fighting peons complied. Holten swung his arm downward in an arc, indicating the far slope. There they had protective fire from the snipers. He set spurs to Sonny's heaving flanks and led the way out of the mercenary camp.

Reins and bits in hand, several of Iron Mike's men ran to their horses. Hasty pursuit was organized under command of Bob Snow. Singly, then in pairs and threes, the mercenaries streamed after the withdrawing peons. The distance separating them closed rapidly and the free company soldiers opened fire. So intent were they in exacting vengeance that they failed to hear the clear, brassy notes of Corporal Lomalin's bugle.

The boiling dust cloud ahead blew away to reveal the brightly uniformed figures of forty lancers, racing down on the mounted mercenaries at a full gallop. Another spritely flurry of notes and the pennant bedecked lances they bore came down in a ripple, into the horizontal attack position.

The retaliatory attackers tried to rein aside their horses to avoid the lances, but it was too late.

Chapter 19

Dust clouded air, already made thick with the pungent odor of blood and death, masked the terrible sights below. A bloated sun bobbed above the sawtoothed horizon, shedding feeble morning light on the scene of slaughter in the small, circular box canyon. The lancers had disengaged, having ridden beyond the invaders' camp and halted now to reorganize under command of Captain Maldonado. The maneuver offered no respite for the beleagered men on the valley floor.

Eli Holten and José Descalso led another sweep of their peon cavalry through the shattered ranks of the mercenaries.

Men and horses screamed in shared agony. On every side men in white shirts and trousers plied their matchetes, severing arms, hands and heads. Pitiful groans came from the wounded. Others of the irregulars descended on these unfortunates and quickly dispatched them. Try as he might, Eli could not halt the butchery. A high frenzy had seized his volunteer soldiers and they fought with but a single purpose. By acting promptly, Holten managed to save the lives of three mercenaries so they could be interrogated. Even those he had to protect at gunpoint.

"Stay back," he snarled at two determined, glassy-eyed peons. "We need them to question."

"*Morirse, gringo cabrónes!*" one of the irregulars shouted, leaping forward.

Holten laid the barrel of his Remington alongside the bloodlusting peon's head. Metal on bone made a hollow, clonking sound and the attacker stopped with enough suddenness to flip backward off his feet.

"I'll kill the first man who touches these prisoners," the scout coldly told the remaining pair.

In a frozen moment, Eli realized he had been shouting into a complete blanket of silence. The battle had ended. Sweating, panting men gathered around. Their white garments had been dyed a deep crimson, faces and hands heavily spattered and slicked by blood. The clop of a horse's hoofs sounded loud in Eli's ears. Captain Maldonado rode up and saluted smartly.

"It was a magnificent charge, Colonel. We have saved the honor of Mexico. *Muchas gracias.*"

"It's only a beginning, Geraldo. You will have ample opportunity to avenge your homeland when we attack Madonna's main force."

The lancer officer beamed with anticipation. "When will that be?"

"Soon. Right soon, I'm sure. First, though, I want these corpses gathered up and tied over their horses. Double them up where necessary. While that's being done, we'll interrogate these prisoners and see what we can learn. Then we head back toward El Triunfo. I have an unpleasant little surprise for Iron Mike Madonna."

* * *

"What the hell do you mean, 'the patrol all came back dead?'" Iron Mike Madonna shouted, an exquisite rage rising from deep inside. "How could they come back if they're dead?"

"Someone sent them," Bob Masters gulped. "They're tied over their horses, strung together into a column. Sentries spotted 'em about ten minutes ago. Nobody around, just dead men and horses."

"Is . . . is Myron Henshaw among them?" Constance inquired in a halting voice.

Masters nodded. Unbidden tears formed in Constance's eyes and she wiped at them angrily with one fist. Her breast heaved and she struggled to form words. Her color betrayed her mounting fury.

"*Eli Holten!* Goddamn him for ever living. He *was* in La Paz and now he's leading an army of peasants against us. It had to be him."

Iron Mike turned to her. "Why do you say that, Connie? This sort of cruelty is well known to be popular with the Mexican army. Look at what they did at the Alamo."

"That was forty years ago. It has to be Eli Holten, I tell you."

"Whoever it is, an example is going to have to be set," Madonna announced grimly. He turned to his second in command. "Ed, send out enough men to round up thirty-five local citizens. Then organize a firing squad. We're going to execute those sons of bitches as a reprisal."

"Right away, Mike," Robbins agreed heartily. He liked the idea of a mass execution. About time, the way he saw it.

"Women and children, too?" Connie asked expectantly.

"There aren't many men in town," Iron Mike answered. "We'll use what we've got."

Noriego Carvajal had lived sixty-five years. Every minute of every day of that time, he had spent in El Triunfo. He had never seen the world beyond his place of birth and he knew nothing of *gringos* or any other sort of soldiers, save the infrequent visits by members of the garrison at La Paz. The men who lived in town and guarded the silver shipments he did not regard as soldiers. When the rough-talking *gringo soldados* came for him, he was having a breakfast of papaya slices, seasoned with lime juice, corn tortillas and cheese.

The invaders jerked him from his stool and frog-marched him out the door. Behind him, his wife wailed in helpless anguish and shouted prayers to her God, who apparently wasn't going to listen. Carvajal found himself in the midst of a small cluster of older men from the town.

"*Buenos dias, viejo* Noriego," several greeted him politely.

"*Muy buenos,*" he replied, still confused as to the purpose of this rude summons. "What is happening?"

"Do you not know, *viejo?* Someone has killed a lot of the *gringo soldados,*" Brualdo Camacho told him. "Now they are going to make of us something called an example. I don't know what that means, but I don't think I like it very much."

"Perhaps they wish to question us as to who might have done this thing. Maybe to show us the bodies to make us feel shame," another gray-haired man suggested. "They have done little to harm us so far."

Noriego shrugged and a hint of a mocking smile lifted his lips. "Outside of destroying the front of the *Edificio Municipal,* killing maybe forty people and raping our women, executing our priest, Gustavo, they have done little to harm us. *Mierda!* Are you so stupid you do not see these men are evil?"

Gustavo shuffled his huarache-clad feet in the dust. "It is not for us to question the deeds of conquerors," he murmured.

"Then who is to do it?" Noriego asked quietly.

More people joined the assemblage, including tear-stained women and half a dozen big-eyed children, aged from six to eleven. The newcomers asked the same, inevitable questions and received variations of the answers. The sun had begun to grow hot and Noriego resented that the *gringos* had not let him take his hat. From all over town, people began to appear, pushed toward the cluster by armed invaders.

"This is looking worse all the time," Noriego told those around him. "Somehow I do not think they have our interests at heart. Something bad is being planned this day."

Bustling activity filled the place in front of the church at El Triunfo. The mercenaries, speaking English, sounded shrill against the soft background murmur of Spanish voices. With curses, kicks and rifle butts, the invaders shoved a group of some thirty-five persons into a rough semblance of a line. Still prodding and kicking, the heavily armed freebooters marched the people to a spot at one side of the church. There they pointed to the men and older boys. They made gestures indicating that the shovels laying there were to be used.

With more profane English and a few shouted commands in badly accented Spanish, the conquerors of El Triunfo made it clear they wanted a long, wide trench dug. Reluctant to obey, but helpless to protest, the chosen men began to hack at the earth. Slowly, the form of the ditch began to emerge. As the laborers sweated and strained against the hard ground, other peons moved busily around the town.

"What are they doing down there?" José Descalso inquired in a whisper.

"About what I expected," Eli Holten replied.

"It looks like grave diggers gone wild."

"That's what it is." To Descalso's quizzical look, Eli went on. "Madonna is going to have a mass execution as a reprisal for our ambush of his patrol."

"Women and children, too? *Chingado!* He is worse than the French."

"At least it's only one for one. He could make it as bloody as he wanted."

"Small compensation, if you are one of the chosen, no? Why are we doing nothing about it?"

"Wait. That's all we can do."

Nearly an hour passed before the ditch had been completed. Sweating and dirty, the diggers were prodded into line with the other townspeople, their backs to the trench. A dozen mercenaries came forward and began to tie the captives' hands behind their backs. Realization dawned on some of them and a pitiful lamentation rose as many of the men and women began to pray. Others cursed their executioners and spat at them. Two men at the far end of the line attempted to make a break.

Swiftly, guards closed in and clubbed them into submission with rifle butts. A command barked out from around at the front of the church and forty riflemen came into view, weapons shouldered. They marched in two files, which halted abreast of the condemned.

"De-tail . . . Left . . . face!" the leader of the firing party ordered. "Pre-sent . . . arms! . . . Port . . . arms! . . . With three rounds, load and lock! . . . First rank . . . kneel! Second rank stand fast! . . . Ready! . . . Aim! . . ."

That final, fateful word never left his mouth. What sound of it may have existed got lost in the ear-disabling roar of exploding dynamite.

The first charges went off less than twenty feet from the firing squad. Men were knocked from their feet and a few wild shots crackled skyward, or into the ground. Before the stunning effect of the blasting powder could dissipate, more bursts erupted throughout town. Horses and other livestock whinnied and shrieked in panic. Mercenaries ran from place to place, confused, their minds and bodies pounded by the force of the explosions. Then members of the execution detail began to drop and rifle fire could be heard rattling amid further outbursts of blasting powder. Iron Mike Madonna ran into the street, shouting orders and curses.

"Get mounted up! Go after those bastards! You blind sons of bitches, they got the jump on you again!"

"Some of 'em are right here in town," Ed Robbins yelled in Madonna's ear as another blast ripped the cornice from a grocery store on the main street.

Flying pieces of masonry cleared two freebooters out of their saddles. Ringed by snipers, more of the tall, easily distinguished *gringos* staggered and fell bleeding into the thirsty soil as bullets cracked through the air in every direction. Riderless horses added to the tumult. A corral side shattered and braying, wild-eyed burros swarmed among the scurrying mercenaries.

"Now," Eli Holten commanded.

Two dozen picked men ran down the near slope to the side of the church. Half their number stood careful watch, while the remainder cut the bonds of the would-be victims. While they worked, Madonna's artillery at last opened up. Roundshot from the six pounders howled through the air to burst in fountains of dust against the arid hills. Several mercenaries saw the rescue attempt in progress and aimed their rifles toward the knot of people around the fresh trench.

Three of them died instantly as the rifles in the hands of *caballeros* and ex-soldiers spat deadly accurate fire. Here a head became a misty ball of crimson froth. There a freebooter staggered about drunkenly, his life's blood pumping from a huge exit wound in his back. The attackers closed ranks and prepared to make their withdrawal.

One of those to be executed gave a wild cry and pitched sideways into the mass grave. An irregular groaned and clutched at a spreading wound in his right side. Undaunted the entire party continued toward safety in the mountains. A four pounder skidded around a corner and the men hauling it spun into position.

Fear seized the townspeople and they ran from their rescuers. Swiftly the crew serviced the little cannon and made ready to lay a slow match on the touch hole. Three straw-hatted peons rose from behind the parapet of the closest building and hurled the smoke-trailing objects in their hands.

Bracketed in a triangle, the little gun flew off its carriage when the dynamite exploded. Firing dwindled gradually along the ridges around El Triunfo. With fewer targets, confusion reclaimed the mercenaries. Incaution, however, did not come with it.

"Go on," Iron Mike snarled. "Get moving, damnit! Go after those prisoners who escaped."

Hesitant and nervous, ten horsemen started out from the cover of a large adobe livery barn. They clattered out of town and started upslope at the point where the last of the fleeing townspeople disappeared. They made fifty yards, when the grade in front of them belched greasy powder smoke.

Four men toppled from the mounts' backs and the other horses went wild. Stamping, snorting and prancing, the frightened animals gave the six survivors all they could do to retain their seats. While disorder persisted, figures rose to swing machetes at the men's exposed legs, arms and the heads of the skitterish beasts. Two of the remaining freebooters managed to break free.

They turned aside to see an aparition straight out of the pit rise before them.

Knife in his left hand, held low and level, primed to plunge upward and disembowel, smoking Remington in his right, Eli Holten stood from among the rocks. His face was begrimed with powder smoke and a wild light glowed in his steely gray eyes. His mouth twisted in a contorted shape as he yelled defiance at the men he confronted.

"Yeaaaagh!"

Instantly, he fired his revolver. The bullet smoked hot but harmless past the left ear of one mercenary. The force of its passing rattled the adventurer for a moment and he missed his chance to finish their nemesis. His partner, though, got off a shot.

Enormous pain exploded in the scout's belly, as Eli Holten slammed back against a huge brown boulder. The Remington flew from his hand as new agony erupted in his back. All the air gusted from his lungs and pinpoints of blackness expanded into huge balloons before his eyes. Dimly he perceived Madonna's soldier taking aim for another shot.

Mustering all his rapidly draining strength, Eli lifted his Bowie and hurled it at his tormentor. The blade-heavy weapon made a single turn in the air, slid in under the mercenary's gun arm and buried to the hilt in the soft flesh of his belly. His right arm jerked involuntarily and the slug went high, screaming as it chipped rock on the big boulder against which Holten lay spread-eagled.

A soft sigh escaped the invader's thick lips. He heaved his chest in an attempt to preserve what rapidly drained away. Then, with another moan, he slumped forward on his horse's neck. The six-gun dropped from his lifeless fingers.

Holten dived for the revolver as the other freebooter blasted a bullet in his direction. The scout did a shoulder roll, his body still aching and weak, and came up with the trembling muzzle of the .45 Colt pointed in the direction of the remaining gunman. With all his energy, he struggled to hold the six-gun still as he fired one shot, cocked and let off another, then a third.

His first slug struck the horse in its broad chest. It whinnied pitifully, trembled and began to sag in the foreknees. The second bullet smashed the elbow of the mercenary. He howled with pain and shock for a fraction of a minute before the third round blew off the back of his head. Satisfied, the scout turned away.

Immense pain and heavy weariness filled him and Holten's body quivered with icy chills. He took a tottering step before blackness descended over him like one of the mighty waves he had seen during the hurricane.

Chapter 20

"I told you it had to be Eli Holten," Constance snapped when Iron Mike had summoned his staff for an evaluation of the attack. "He was in La Paz, he sent those dead men to us and I saw him again during the fighting."

Irregular forces had withdrawn from El Triunfo some fifteen minutes earlier. Wise in the ways of partisan fighters, Madonna had not sent men in pursuit. Instead, he set them to taking the final toll on the battle which had so swiftly descended on the mining town.

"Where did you see Holten?" Madonna asked intently.

"On the slope behind the smelter. Near the end of fighting, he was with their, ah, rear guard. I think one of your men finished him off though."

Ed Robbins opened the door to admit two grim-faced mercenaries. They held a whispered conversation for several seconds, then Ed stepped to the table where Madonna had laid out crude maps of the area.

"Bad news, Mike. We've sustained over a hundred twenty casualties. Sixty-three dead, about fifteen more who won't make it through to tomorrow, and the rest wounded. Of those, twenty are injured too seriously to be moved. The rest are the usual scrapes and scratches."

"Shit!" Madonna exploded. "How long will we be delayed by this?"

"Hard saying," Ed answered candidly. "We could leave the badly wounded under guard and move out by first light tomorrow. If we wait for them to improve . . ." He canted his head to one side in a negative gesture. "We could be here another month. One good thing, though. Most of those killed were among the bandits who have joined us."

"Hummm. In which case, we still maintain our basic strength. How about the smelter? Any damage?"

"None," one of the detachment commanders informed him.

"Then our repairs make us ready to start processing ore. We'd planned to leave enough force here to oversee the mining and smelting and maintain order. That should be sufficient to protect the wounded. What we need . . ." Madonna smashed a fist onto the top map, over the bay of La Paz. "What we need is to find some of these partisans, execute them, then push on and finish this thing. Once we've taken La Paz, we can concentrate on any guerrillas who remain. That's what we'll do then. Notify all detachment commanders and squad leaders. Full provisions, field packs and all gear are to be made ready within twenty-four hours, along with everyone able to sit a horse or march. Have patrols organized and sent out to scour the country within ten leagues of El Triunfo for partisans. They are to find them and bring them back here and hang them. Then, we march on La Paz."

Too-bright light backgrounded fuzzy, out-of-focus

patterns of leaves. Agony surged in waves from the middle of his stomach. He couldn't be dead, Eli Holten decided. If so, he wouldn't hurt so damned much. Distorted human forms moved into his foggy field of vision and voices boomed like stentorian shouts.

"He is awake, *mí doña.*"

My lady? Who the hell? And more important, where are we? Holten wanted to know the answers before he risked moving or trying to sit up.

"*Gracias,* Ramon."

Holten rejected the evidence of his unreliable senses. Carmella Morales? Was he in La Paz?

"Eli. Eli, can you speak?"

It *was* Carmella. Holten groaned. He worked his lips and throat. Only croaking sounds emerged.

"How . . . how long have I been unconscious?" he finally managed.

"Not long. Two or three minutes the first time, they tell me. Then about an hour. We are near the caves where my brothers established the camp."

That answered two questions, only to create another. "What are you doing here?"

"I asked you in La Paz, remember? You said no, but I knew you meant yes. I belong with those fighting for our freedom."

"Oh . . . shit!" Holten groaned in English.

"You make it sound better in Spanish. *Mierda!* But that is of no matter. I am here and I will stay."

"No you won't," the scout fired back.

He attempted to rise, then fell back in a spasm of pain. Carmella's soft hands were on his bare chest. "You are hurt," she told him softly, as though that answered everything. "I will nurse you."

Holten looked down the long, rangy length of his body, noting a tinge of yellow-purple bruise above bands of white cloth wrapped around his middle. He turned his head at the sound of footsteps to look at José Ramon Descalso.

"You are lucky, *amigo*. That bullet smashed into your buckle and the double layer of your belt. Only the tip broke skin an inch above your navel."

"You are bruised and you'll be sore for some while," Angel Morales added as he walked to the narrow bunk where Eli lay. "Even so, you will be able to fight again before the week is out."

"That's . . . comforting to know," the scout replied with less than total enthusiasm. "What is Madonna doing?"

"We don't know as yet," Angel informed him. "We have scouts out, there are others who work for Morales ranches, friendly watchers to bring word. It has been but three hours since we left El Triunfo."

"Then we'll know soon enough," Holten predicted.

A sudden, brisk shower fell from an impossibly tiny cloud, drenching the partisans before they entered the cave. Off to the west, huge ramparts of black, muddy gray and white blotted out the sky.

"Another big storm is coming," Roberto Morales told the scout. "Perhaps even a *chirabusco.*"

"I can do without another hurricane, thank you."

"Carmella is fixing you some hot soup. It's goat meat, but it is good."

Holten suppressed a smile. "For which I'm grateful."

More astute and reflective than his brothers, Roberto

studied Holten's face. He strummed a few random chords on his guitar. "You look troubled."

"I am, and not just about being punched in the belly by a bullet. Our attack on El Triunfo may trigger Madonna into action again. He might set out for La Paz sooner than expected. We have to be ready and so does the army. The key to destroying him is to catch his troops in the open, between our two forces."

"And the soldiers don't know what we have done."

"Exactly."

"I could go to them, tell them everything."

Holten brightened. "Good idea. The man to see is Colonel Armando Hurtado. You met him in La Paz. Go to the same office and tell him what has happened and what we suspect may be next. Do it now. Don't wait another hour."

"*Sí, Jefe.*" Roberto grinned. "My brothers think they are the leaders. I know it to be another way. Rest and get well. I will leave for La Paz at once."

Carmella brought the soup and Eli ate it with increasing appetite. He drowsed through the afternoon, storing energy and letting his body heal its disorders. The bruise would last a long time, as would the small hole where the bullet had penetrated his skin. Most of his soreness, though, had departed by nightfall. Brooding thunder rumbled on the far horizon an hour later, when Carmella came to his darkened portion of the interlocking caverns.

"You will not send me back. I know it," she breathed in his ear. "I heard what you said about the *gringo*, Madonna, attacking La Paz. It would be safer here."

"But, Carmella . . ."

Holten stopped at the soft rustle of cloth. He heard

Carmella's heavy breathing and sensed her close return. Bare skin brushed over his own and, despite his injury, heat glowed in his loins, tendrils seeping out through his body. A slight pressure told him of Carmella's fingers at his waistband. In a moment, his rising organ tingled to the coolness of the cave's atmosphere.

"Here now," Carmella cautioned. "Let me do everything. You are wounded. But not too sick, I think to, ah, enjoy what is offered."

Bass grumblings drew closer as a huge storm developed outside. Carmella climbed onto the bed, astraddle of the scout and reached out with both hands to encompass the rapidly expanding fullness of his pulsing maleness. She squeezed and kneaded it, urging new life into the hot, silken flesh. Holten touched the inner surfaces of her thighs and stroked them lightly. Little shivers of delight coarsed through both of them. Slowly the squatting girl lowered herself until the broad, flat tip of his engorged phallus pressed into the fronds of her antichamber.

She wriggled about then, moistening the mighty lance with ample of her free-flowing nectar, then invited the further inspection of her palace of desire. Pulses of electric sensation transported the scout far from the pain of reality. By the most minute of increments, Carmella welcomed him deep within her humid atrium and beyond to the inner sanctum of her being.

If only convalescence could always be like this, Eli thought as he surrendered himself to what he knew would be a long night of exquisite passion.

Chapter 21

Relentless desert sun beat down on the long column as it moved out of the mountains into the dune-humped desert foothills that spread fan-like toward the Bay of La Paz, some fourteen miles away. Great dark rings, their edges white with mineral incrustations, extended below the arm pits of every freebooter's shirt. Not even Milo Madonna had escaped the harshness of the inhospitable terrain.

His dark thoughts didn't help the climate any. He had come to regret leaving men and many supplies behind in El Triunfo. Particularly when his patrols had discovered nothing and returned unharmed and empty-handed. He knew the remnants of the partisan force lurked in those steep folds and gulleys of the mountains around the silver mining town. His lines of communication and supply stretched thinner with every passing mile. Constance Williams cantered up beside him and matched the slow pace he had adopted, dictated by the maximum safe speed of the artillery. He turned his head toward her and made an attempt at a smile.

"We haven't made a mile in the last two hours," Constance complained.

"It would kill those draft animals on the caissons," Madonna informed her.

She looked terrible, he appraised. Deep lines creased her forehead out of grief for Henshaw's death and in ill-suppressed anger for the failure of the retaliatory executions. Her nose, eyes and the corners of her mouth were pinched white with the strain. Her auburn hair had gone straggly, stray wisps blowing in the hot breeze that sucked the moisture from their exposed skin. Only fury seemed to drive her. Madonna decided to try to draw her out.

"You've never told me why it really was that you took such unusual pleasure in killing that priest in Todos Santos? Are you a fallen Catholic?"

Startled by this new line, Constance let go her pent-up emotions. A variety of expressions rippled across her countenance before she gave a light trill of laughter and reached out to pat Madonna's gloved hand.

"Oh, heavens no. Far from that. I don't really know." She screwed her face up as though in deep, serious thought. Her words, when they came at last, had a flavor of being carefully selected. They described images culled from her past. Her revelations had a chilling effect on Milo Madonna.

"It's a part of this strange craving I have for sex. I can't stand a man who isn't a man . . . if that makes any sense. A priest is celibate. A eunuch. He doesn't even radiate the sort of aura and musky smell of a *real* man. I get all cold around him. That . . . and a sort of rage."

"You keep saying, 'him,' instead of they. Why is that?"

For a long half a minute, Constance remained silent, a stunned expression on her face. Drained of color, her cheeks suddenly suffused with scarlet. Tears formed in her eyes.

"I . . . well, it happened a long time ago. Back when I was only fourteen. I had the hots all the time, since a boarder in my mother's establishment initiated me the year before. Among those I chose to offer my charms to—ah, to relieve my itch, so's to speak—was the priest at the church in our town. I thought . . . you know . . . a man who lived without women would be in as much need as I. Uh, he, uh, watched me trying to be seductive and listened to the words I said, words that got cruder as I got hotter and he made no response. Then . . . at last, he told me how sorry he was to see a sweet little girl go so wrong. He said he would pray for me and that I should pray to the Virgin Mary for strength and forgiveness.

"It made me furious. I swore at him and tried to strike him. I cried while I ran all the way home. If George, the boarder I mentioned, hadn't been there to comfort me, to take me to bed, I don't know what I would have done. Now, I've said it all, though I thought I had forgotten it over the years. Then, there in Todos Santos, I saw this priest who had been leading the fighting against our men. I saw it as a chance to express what I felt."

"And did you find it all to your liking?"

Constance paled slightly and swatted at a cluster of tiny, black insects that hovered around her face. "To be honest . . . no. Afterward, I wondered, ah, if God would punish me for what I had done." She swung an open hand at the buzzing, irritating midges. "Ugh! I'll be glad when we're off this desert."

"Two more days and we'll know for sure. The Mexican army will either come out and fight us or they'll abandon La Paz and sail away shouting curses."

"I hope it won't be the first of those options."

"In a way it would be to our advantage if it were. Much better to defeat them. That way it would give us more time before any larger force could be sent against us."

Birds chirped in the stunted trees of the town. In the distance, tiny bells tinkled and goats bleated flatly, herded by small boys from El Triunfo. The air had that special brightness that follows a clean washing by a large, violent storm. Puddles stood in the streets and yards. The peace and tranquillity of the place made Gaston Fouchet think of his boyhood home in the Pyrenees Mountains of southwest France. Gaston sighed, recalling how short a time his childhood had been.

He had fought in some army, for some cause, since the age of fifteen. First, with his Basque cousins against the Spanish, then the French. Those rugged mountains had been *theirs*, did not belong to the men from Madrid or Paris. Later, under an assumed name, he waged war against the Riff in the desert of North Africa, serving in the Foreign Legion of the French. How ironic, he often told himself. After his enlistment, he did battle for other countries in Africa, then returned to the Legion.

Which brought him to Mexico to prop up the tottering regime of the Austrian, Maximilian. He had barely escaped that fiasco with his life. The rest of his command had been wiped out at a place called Camerón. He found, though, that he liked the New World and remained, serving one petty dictator after another in the pseudo-countries of Central America. Until he met Iron Mike Madonna. He signed on eagerly with the free company and found a new, better way to be a soldier. Until they came to this small town in the mountains of Baja California, at least.

It seemed far too much like home. Sheep and goats abounded, with few cattle or planted crops. Brown skinned, barefoot boys tended the flocks and dark-eyed girls walked the rocky mountain paths with the same swaying grace of his own village of Prats-de-Mollo, in the Basque country. He'd like to live here, raise a family, not come as a conqueror, to be hated and feared. At least the duty wasn't hard, Gaston acknowledged.

They were forty in number. Iron Mike had left them behind to care for the wounded, supervise the silver mines and smelter, protect provisions and provide lines of supply and communication with the main force. Gaston partly wished he could have gone along, to see the big city of La Paz and get wet in the warm waters of the Sea of Cortez. The wiser, old soldier part of him knew he had the best of all possible duty.

His share of the loot was guaranteed by Iron Mike. He had been promoted, first to *sous-officier*, then to lieutenant. It had been more by merit than attrition, Gaston liked to think. Now he could take it easy and enjoy the privilege of rank. With a prodigious yawn and stretch, he roused himself from where he sat under a spreading live oak. Another bend and twist to loosen the kinked muscles and he started down toward the town.

Gaston made a hundred yards before a huge hand snaked around his face and clamped tightly over his mouth. He had time to register a momentary panic and bloom of regret before the white-hot agony of a wide, thick blade slid through his flesh and destroyed his left kidney.

Numbed by shock, Gaston could only quiver while the

steel wrecked its fearful destruction among his vitals. Tears formed in his green eyes as he went rigid when the knife came away with an ugly sucking sound. The powerful figure behind him shifted position and the Bowie once more pierced Gaston's back. The Basque soldier's right kidney destroyed, his consciousness exploded in a widening sphere of blackness that quickly engulfed him.

Oh . . . oh . . . oh, to be in my beautiful Prats-de-Mollo, Gaston lamented as his body went slack and he slipped into the eternal pit of death.

Eli Holten lowered the corpse of the mercenary lieutenant to the ground. He bent and wiped his blood-smeared hands and his Bowie clean on Gaston's shirt. The scout turned slightly and gave a silent arm signal to the crouching guerrillas who waited for him to remove this threat to their surprise. Flowing with the deadly, frightening grace of a prairie fire, the long, three-deep lines rippled down the slope, closing rapidly on the nearer buildings.

Fifty paces became thirty, then twenty . . . ten. A not-too-alert sentry stared gape-mouthed at the huge tide of men descending on the town and far too late, shouldered his rifle and fired a shot.

A thunderous volley answered him. Torn to shreds, his limp body flung away from the parapet of the municipal building in bits and pieces. So much for the element of surprise, Holten thought. Though in fact, their objective had been reached. Peons and Angel's Yaquis swarmed through the streets of El Triunfo. They kicked in doors, blasted away with their rifles and hurried on to find more victims. Eli led a picked group toward the smelter.

A low adobe wall surrounded the grounds of the twin-stacked smelter. There, mercenaries knelt and fired accurately on the attackers. A peon screamed and pitched forward to sprawl in a mud puddle. Another grunted and swerved to the side, to crash into a fellow guerrilla before surrendering to mortality. Bullets moaned and cracked through the air, some so close the scout needed only to cant his head to one side or the other to be mortally wounded. Still he pressed on.

"At them!" he commanded. "Fire by volley. Press in, press in!"

"They are so many," Miguel, the apprentice scout declared from Eli's left.

"Only to be expected," Holten assured him. "This is the place they'd most want to protect. Keep going."

Barrels, boulders and hummocks of earth became makeshift parapets as half the men fired in volley and the remainder rushed forward to the next shelter and repeated the process for their comrades. When the charging line reached throwing distance, Holten raised his arm high and, oblivious to the storm of lead that snapped around him, remained motionless in plain sight.

"Now!" he commanded.

Ten men dropped out of the attack formation, knelt and touched glowing cigar stubs to the frizzled ends of black fuse. Their eyes fixed on the scout, they waited for his signal.

"Throw!" Eli shouted in Spanish, his arm whipping downward.

Ten sticks of blasting powder arched through the pearly morning sky. They landed scant inches behind the adobe wall. Several mercenaries shouted their alarm and tried to run away. Shattering roars filled the streets of El Triunfo as the explosive packages detonated.

Dust and smoke obscured the savaged area and the moans and wails of injured men washed over the attackers. Many of the peons, unused to the effect of dynamite, stood in blank-faced astonishment.

"At them, *compañeros!*" Holten shouted. "Get them all!"

With fearsome shouts, the partisans surged forward and vaulted the wall. Terrible shrieks were cut off by the meaty smack of machetes. Heads rolled, arms dropped uselessly from the bodies of shock-frozen mercenaries and the sweet, cloying odor of bloody death filled Holten's nostrils.

"Search the buildings. Then we move on to meet up with Descalso's detachment," Holten instructed.

Where did they all come from? The question demanded answer, though Bill Clay could give no time to it. He and three other mercenaries busily pursued a more important goal—getting away with their lives. Clay felt the hot breath of a bullet, as it whipped close past his cheek a fraction of a second before he heard the report. Involuntarily, he jumped to the left.

Running next to him, Stuart Mills gave a harsh grunt and lurched forward to fall on his face. Sharp-edged bits of decomposed granite—which formed much of the sand of the mountainous desert—cut and gouged flesh away from bone before the dying mercenary stopped skidding. Clay winced in sympathy and continued to churn his legs. The more distance he put between him and the partisans in El Triunfo, the better.

"Lars, Thad, over this way," he panted. "Get those hills between us and the town and we'll be safe."

Swiftly, the surviving trio sprinted toward the sheltering protection of the low, sandy hills. Bill Clay's lungs ached, his breath, hot and raspy, scraped at his throat. Every footfall put him further away from the murderous fire that came from every part of El Triunfo. Sand kicked up behind him and the richochet moaned overhead. Only a little further.

Head down, every muscle striving, Bill Clay led the other survivors onward. The ground rose under his feet. Ahead lay safety. Only a dozen more steps. The staccato sound of constant gunfire behind them had faded to an insistent crackle. Closer now. Only a few more seconds.

Bill Clay came over the rise and skidded to a horrified halt. Eyes bugged and mouth opened to scream a denial, he looked at the awesome sight he had uncovered.

Resplendent in their gaudy green-white-and-red uniforms, a dozen *lanceros* sat their mounts across the path taken by Bill Clay and his fellow mercenaries. Bright gold and green ribbon pennants rippled at the base of the broad, shiny steel blades of their lances. At a barked command, the long, wooden spears rippled down into line.

"*Lanceros . . . ASALTAN!*" the sergeant commanding the splendidly outfitted soldiers bellowed.

"Oooooh! Shiiiit!" Bill Clay, filled with deep conviction of his impending destruction, screamed a moment before the leaf-shaped steel blade of a lance head cleaved through his ribcage and burst his heart.

"You two, break to the left," Eli Holten told the peons at his side. "You come with me. The rest of you wait here and give us covering fire."

Determined and competent resistance had formed up around a nucleus of mercenary non-coms who had taken over a *pulqueria* on the main street of El Triunfo. They had the intention of emptying the establishment's stock in trade of the bitter, odorous fermented cactus juice in one day. Instead, they found themselves in the midst of a small war. When the first shock of the unexpected attack waned, several grimly purposeful mercenaries fought their way to the hole-in-the-wall saloon.

Protected on both sides and the rear by other thick-walled, cubical-like business establishments, the *pulqueria* became a sturdy fort, easily defended from frontal assault. At least until the scout arrived with his men after taking the smelter.

"Keep your heads down after I throw," Holten advised his troops.

He held a bundle of three sticks of dynamite in his right hand. One of his slim, dry-cured cigars protruded from the left corner of his mouth. Its tip glowed a cherry red behind a thick, gray segment of ash. Holten removed the stogie and blew on the end. He touched it to the frayed fuse as he spoke again.

"After the explosion, run like hell toward the front. Fire all the way, fast as you can. Ready?"

Sober-visaged heads nodded. Holten blew on the bright fire of the fuse and watched as it caught. A thin wisp of smoke rose from the black-tarred powder train. He watched while half the length burned away. Then he gestured with his left hand, cigar extended like a schoolmaster's pointer.

"You three, open fire. Cover me."

Fat .45-70 slugs cracked through the air and slammed into the shattered doorway of the shop. Eli Holten rose from behind the overturned *carreta* and gauged his distance. Then he brought his arm back and hurled the heavy parcel toward the same opening.

With a final curl of smoke, it disappeared inside.

The ferocious blast opened the gates of hell inside the drinking establishment. Its front bulged and spilled into the street as crumbled rubble, amid billows of smoke and dust. With it came the end of all resistance in El Triunfo. Screams began as the merciless Yaqui Indians, led by the Morales brothers, started killing the wounded mercenaries.

Iron Mike Madonna no longer had a relief force, nor supplies nor anyone to carry or receive messages. Now the real fight would begin, the scout thought grimly.

Chapter 22

La Paz still remained an impossible-seeming thirteen miles away when another day dawned. The bivouac rose slowly, desert lethargy sapping the men and animals. Cookfires were lighted and hours wasted repacking animals for another short stint of four miles. While the work progressed, Milo Madonna walked to the edge of camp, to look back down the road toward El Triunfo.

A terrible premonition seized him. One so vivid and immediate that it didn't surprise him when the apparition of a man appeared. Moments went by in total silence while the figure in tattered clothing grew closer, more substantial. Not a spirit, Madonna decided, a real man.

Wounded, dirty, reeling from lack of food, blood and sleep, the stubble-faced mercenary stumbled up to report to Iron Mike.

"Took the town, Cap'n. The whole damned place is in th-the hands of the greasers."

The words drove a shaft of ice through Madonna's heart. "I'd heard some firing yesterday. Thought it might be a small probe to test your strength. What about Gaston? Lieutenant Fouchet?"

"He died at the first. They are all dead. Killed with

rifles and dynamite, many with the long knives, machetes. All dead. Oh, Christ! All but me."

"Let me get you some water. How many attacked you?" The coldness in the pit of his stomach told Iron Mike that he had irrevocably lost El Triunfo.

"About two hundred fifty, maybe more. They looked like partisans, but they fought like regulars. Even had lancers with them."

"The army?" Iron Mike asked, worried anew.

"They could have been."

Madonna's blue eyes clouded as he weighed the situation. Two-fifty to three hundred against forty? There would be no one to turn back and rescue. The loss of his supplies and forty good men hurt badly. Now he had no choice but to advance. Still, the Mexican army had not been seen anywhere except perhaps for this. If they went on, left the greaser army at their backs. . . . If they took La Paz with little resistance, he could then send a large detachment to deal with the army and any number of partisans. Madonna led the man to a cookfire and saw that he had water first, then hot coffee and food. Iron Mike went off then, thinking dark, private thoughts.

The soldier's report had been more a disappointment than a surprise. He had expected some sort of activity around El Triunfo. Not such an overwhelming force, though. Where could all of those partisans come from? He summoned Ed Robbins and his best scout.

"Trouble, Mike?" Ed Robbins asked as he walked up, reading the emotions that played across his superior's face.

"And then some. El Triunfo has fallen to a large force of enemy."

"Partisans again?"

"Or the army. We don't know. I want you to make sure everything is loaded and ready to depart the head of the column immediately after breakfast. We have to reach La Paz the day after tomorrow some time. Now then, Barton," Madonna went on, addressing his scout.

He wanted to tell him to send out several well-armed patrols to check on the conditions in El Triunfo and to insure the security of the flanks. Before he could do so, however, Madonna received his third rude surprise of the day.

The tracker's body slammed forward until he crashed into Milo Madonna. The pair clung together a moment in a macabre embrace before the younger man's knees gave way and he slid down Iron Mike's chest. Terrible damage had been done to Seth Barton's back by a nearly spent .45-70-405 bullet. It entered his body sideways and did worse harm to his lungs. Blood gushed from Barton's mouth and splattered all over Iron Mike's shirt.

"There's a sniper out there!" Madonna yelled as he dove away from the shambles.

"We have to make them move," Eli Holten declared as he and Carlos Ocampo studied the free company in its camp five hundred yards distant.

"Why not hold them here? You sent Roberto Morales for the troops. If our snipers can keep them in a defensive position we can eventually surround them and finish it in a single blow."

"*If* General Alleman decides to move on the recommendation of a Yaqui Indian. With this army of mercenaries only thirteen miles from town, the generals ought to do something. Only . . ."

"I wonder, too, *amigo*. Eli, haven't we enough men, with our volunteers, the Morales' Yaquis and the lancers, to do it ourselves?"

"Yes," the scout admitted hesitantly. "And of them, only the lancers and a handful of others have any formal military training. In a frontal assault, across open ground, Madonna's artillery would eat them up. Those at least who didn't run. We have to wait, but we can't afford to. That's why I want Madonna's troops strung out in a column. The only thing to do is pull back and let them get moving."

Carlos snorted. "Many of our men will feel that is cowardly."

"There isn't time for *machismo*, Carlos. The standing rule is that irregulars don't fight pitched battles."

"They'll do anything if you order it," Carlos suggested.

"Then let 'em draw back and give Madonna a chance to get on the march again."

Angel Morales cursed with impatience. Would the *gringo* soldiers never get to the right spot on the road? Why must it be he and his Yaquis who waited for them? Angel looked over to where Holten sat calmly, a small pen knife in one hand, whittling a dried stalk of occatillo cactus. A half-smoked cigar jutted from the corner of the American scout's mouth. Hiding and waiting. Angel grunted with resignation. He would have to endure it. After all, his ancestors had done it the same way he'd been told. A moment later, he stiffened and gazed intently to the southwest.

From his vantage point, on one of the high hills that bounded the main road to La Paz, Angel peered at the horizon. Through the ripples of heat haze, he discerned bulky movement. Indistinct forms wavered in and out of focus. The *gringo* army! He made silent hand signals and his Yaqui fighting men disappeared into the hillside. With a snort of disgust, Angel realized that Holten had also done so, only sooner than his men. An ant crawled past Angel's eyes, magnified by his closeness. Time moved slower than the insect.

At last the column drew abreast of the ambush site. In the lead rode Iron Mike Madonna and the woman Holten had called a devil. Angel thought it an apt description. No wonder it had taken so long. They walked their horses. Nothing moved faster than the ponderous carts on which the cannon rested. What easy targets these foreign invaders made. Angel chaffed at the restraint he imposed when the head of the column could so easily be attacked. A smile at last creased his leathered face as he saw the sputtering smoke of fuses across the road on the opposite hill. Soon now, he promised himself.

Fifty of Madonna's soldiers remained in the narrow defile when the dynamite went off. Tons of boulders, rocks and other debris instantly rumbled down on the helpless troops. Men and animals shrieked. Angel came to his feet and rushed downslope with his screaming, blood-lusting warriors.

Eli Holten came with them, only inches behind the last ripple of tumbling sand and rocks. The Remington revolver in his right fist blasted once, twice and a redarmbanded non-com flopped backward against a rill of stone, formed by the slowing rockslide.

"To the front! To the front!" Holten shouted to the Yaquis. "Hold off the others while we finish these men."

Half a dozen Morales miners and ranch hands hurried to comply. Holten grabbed at the shoulder of another and sent him forward also. Over their heads, he fired shots through the curtain of dust at hazy, moving forms. Around him, the sounds of killing went on.

"Angel," the scout called. "Get some more of your men on holding off the rest of the column. There's more'n three hundred soldiers up there."

"It is best," Angel answered tightly.

An injured sergeant reared up suddenly from under a layer of smaller rocks and dirt. His left arm had been shattered by a boulder, the flesh pulped, bone splintered and crushed. It didn't prevent him from using the Starr .44 revolver in his right hand, though.

Searing pain ripped at Angel's guts as the fat ball from the Starr punched into the right side of his rigid abdomen and set him to staggering backward. Face contorted, the Yaqui tried to track his Mandragon copy-Colt onto line as his legs gave way and he fell heavily onto the loose rubble that littered the floor of the defile. Grimacing wickedly, the mercenary cocked his weapon for a second shot.

An instant before he would have placed a fatal bullet in Angel's vulnerable chest, the side of his head splashed outward to carmine the buff colored boulders. Remington smoking, the scout stood over the corpse.

"I . . . *gracias.* I am in your debt," Angel managed to gasp out.

"We can't be losing good leaders this early in the war,"

Eli Holten told him, the faint traces of a smile flickering at the corners of his mouth.

Hoofs clattered on the rocks from ahead. Holten swung around in time to clear one sabre-wielding mercenary off his horse with a .44 slug in the soldier's forehead. The second pressed dangerously close. Eli swung the Remington and squeezed the trigger.

A loud click told the scout the worst. Empty. The enemy trooper raised a short Springfield carbine and sighted at point blank range. Holten saw the jaws of eternity gaping wide in the black hole of the .45-70 saddle gun.

"Here! Take this!" Angel shouted.

Eli half-turned and snagged the duplicate Colt out of the air. Already cocked, he fitted it to his big right hand and squeezed off a fast round.

Struck between the eyes, the mercenary's horse crashed to the ground. The bullet from the Springfield blasted into the hillside, an inch from Eli's head. Dust and smoke swirled around him as Holten cocked the Mandragon and squeezed off directly into the surprised face of the freebooter.

Powder flecks speckled the fortune hunter's cheeks and a grim third eye appeared where his nose had once been. His head snapped backward and a fine mist of blood hung in the air a fraction of a second while his corpse fell from the dead horse.

"Time to pull out of here," Holten suggested to Angel.

Pale and weakened, the Yaqui leader could only nod in agreement.

"The big show comes later," Holten promised as he bent to assist Angel.

"We . . . we finish them then, no?"

"Or the next thing to it. Madonna should be off balance enough now that we'll set him up right where we want him," Eli predicted as he walked his injured comrade to a horse. "By noon tomorrow, there won't be any mercenary army."

Chapter 23

Where had they come from? First the dynamite blasts and then those half-naked savages rising up out of the dirt. More than fifty good men killed. Milo Madonna raged at this insulting challenge to his might. Then he chilled with a fresh recollection.

"Our food!" he bellowed. "All our food supplies were at the rear."

"What are we going to do?" Ed Robbins asked, confused and angry.

"We have to keep moving. Send some men, a burial detail. Have them salvage any food that's still usable."

By shortly after noon, the complete toll of the ambush had been brought in. Sixty-one dead, seventeen wounded, forty-five horses killed. All but a day's supply of food had been contaminated by human urine or a greenish-white powder Madonna recognized as strychnine, a deadly poison used in assaying gold. They'd have that, of course. Miners from El Triunfo. How he wished he had leveled the town and killed everyone in it. The march had been barely resumed when scouts galloped in with more bad news.

"The Mexican army is on the move, Cap'n," one lean,

bronze-faced trailsman informed Madonna.

"How many? Where?"

"Damned near to four hunnerd of 'em. Infantry, artillery, some mounted troops. They marched out of La Paz at sunup. Headin' our way."

Damn! damn! damn! Madonna raged inwardly. Were they working in coordination with the partisans who had hit them in the morning? "Hummm," he stalled. "What sort of time are they making?"

"'Bout like us. Maybe a little faster. I reckon we'd meet up along toward sundown day after tomorrow."

Madonna frowned. "Ed, gather the officers and non-coms. We have to make some changes in plan." He turned back to the man who'd brought him the information.

"Keep in contact with the enemy. I'll send some extra men with you. I want a situation report every four hours."

"Can I pick my own men?"

"Within reason."

"We'll be gone in ten minutes."

After the advance party had departed, Milo Madonna sat down with his officers and non-coms. He had spent long minutes in careful thought and now pointed to the rough map on his legs.

"There's another road to the south of our present position. It's hardly more than a goat path, but it does lead to La Paz. What we need to do is get around the Mexican troops, strike at the city. That way we can demoralize the army, panic the civilians and disrupt the supply lines. It also gives us a stronger position to defend."

"What about this place here?" Ed Robbins asked. His

light, freckled complexion had burned bright pink in the hot desert sun and his auburn hair hung in limp, damp locks that strayed from under his hat.

"They're some hills. Much like . . ." Madonna's voice caught. He gruffly cleared his throat and went on. "Much like the ones we came through this morning. We may throw off the partisans by this move, too."

Ed continued to look at the map. "If this were a reliable map, I'd swear that's a box canyon."

"The trail continues, doesn't it?" Madonna asked the obvious.

"Yes," Ed admitted. "But we've had some bad surprises already, using these Mexican maps."

"Only one way to find out," Iron Mike persisted. "That's by going there. We can make it that far with a three hour forced march. Unless there's some really strong argument against, I say we do it."

Darkness clouded their approach. The large camp lay in quiet. Only a few watchfires burned, with sentries posted at regular intervals. Yaqui cunning led the attacking force past these obstacles with ease. One by one they were eliminated. Silent as any of the stalking Yaquis, Eli Holten ghosted into the perimeter of the bivouac without being detected.

He slipped between the tents of snoring men, circling the non-regulation layout twice to satisfy his curiosity. Three hundred men waited a dozen yards away in the darkness to begin their silent slaughter. Eli located the artillery pieces and noted their positions. A special team would be sent to spike the guns. His task completed, the scout hurried to join the waiting force.

"We can do it any time now," he told Carlos and Pablo Morales. "I've sent José Descalso with some men to spike the cannons. Try to make the kills quiet. By the time shooting starts, we want to have reduced the odds by a good lot."

"My men know. Knives and machetes," Pablo whispered back.

"The lancers are ready," Lieutenant Maldonado declared as he stepped close to the meeting, nearly invisible in the stygian blackness of the moonless night. "They are to attack last, Eli?"

"As per plan. Unless something goes seriously wrong. There'll be no way of signaling you, Geraldo, so I'll leave it to your judgement to decide on that. Shall we make it a long count of two hundred and send the first of our troops in?"

A murmur of agreement came from the gathered commanders.

Iron Mike Madonna couldn't sleep. A powerful, pervading sense of foreboding kept him restless and in ill sorts. He had even sent Constance Williams to her tent rather than enjoy her ample and able charms as he had taken to doing recently. He had good cause, Madonna fumed as he rolled on his bunk.

The area between sharply rising hills had indeed proven to be a box canyon. Only a narrow, switch-back trail led up a sheer face of rock to continue the road to La Paz. The artillery caissons would have to be disassembled and transported on pack animals, the tubes wrapped in protective mats and dragged, in order to get them up at all. He could only hope that neither the Mexican army or the partisans discovered his precarious condition. Time for a guard change, Madonna summoned the thought to break off his gloomy introspection.

He raised from his sleepless bed, slid into trousers and boots, then struck a sulfurous lucifer. With its light he checked the large turnip watch which lay on an ammunition case beside his bed, then ignited a cigar. As an afterthought, he belted a holstered revolver around his waist and stepped out into the black night.

It took only a fleeting moment to realize something had drastically changed in the past few seconds. An owl had hooted earlier. Now its mournful query had been replaced with silence. The insects and other night creatures no longer made their familiar music. The timid call of tiny nightbirds had hushed. An electric sense of danger crackled in the air around him.

Madonna nearly shouted an alarm, but other sounds exerted themselves. A rustle of canvas, what might have been a brief scuffle, the meaty smack of steel against flesh, a stifled groan, all repeated a score of times over the next rushing second. The compound impression revealed to him the horrible truth.

The enemy was right there in camp.

Silently the partisans went about murdering his men. Milo Madonna strode purposefully toward two men seated at a watchfire. When he drew nearer, he could clearly see that both had their throats slit. A sudden agonized scream announced a bungled kill. Instantly the camp came awake.

"Guerrillas! In the camp," Madonna shouted. "Rally around me, men!"

Out in the darkness, a rifle spat and the bullet cracked past close to Madonna's left ear. He dodged and continued to exhort his soldiers.

Damn! That scream had alerted the camp, Eli Holten acknowledged. Winchester in hand he stepped into a rough company street, formed by irregularly aligned tents and blasted a barefoot mercenary into the next world. Hampered slightly by the heavy pair of saddlebags over his left shoulder, he quickly cycled the lever action, and point-shot at another freebooter who barged from his tent, six-gun fisted and ready.

Holten's slug smacked into his bare chest and he looked down stupidly at the puckered hole that began to ooze blood. Realizing he had been shot in the lung, the man uttered a pitiful groan and sat on the ground. Large tears began to run down his face, while his chest wound sucked and bubbled. Holten paused long enough to take the revolver from the doomed man's hand.

From the darkness, more rifles opened up.

"Get to the cannon!" Iron Mike's voice bellowed. "Open up on the bastards."

From the far side of the encampment, Holten heard the rhythmic clinking as Descalso's detail drove spikes into the touch holes of Madonna's field pieces. They'd not be doing any firing this night.

"Form up and return fire, for Christ's sake!" Iron Mike boomed.

Holten headed in the direction of the commanding voice. If he could get Madonna, much of their task would be completed.

"Eli, over here!" Carlos Ocampo's voice sought for him from the darkness. "We ran into some heavy resistance."

"On my way," the scout called out.

Figures in full dress, some partially nude, and others bent in the agony of dying, writhed in the flickering light of the bonfires. All of the partisans wore white bands on their hats or around their heads for quick identification. Any who lacked this badge of recognition rapidly died. Sudden movement to his left turned the scout.

A man hurtled out of a ragged tear in one side of a tent. He held a knife now, the edge outward, tip up. He howled in fury and rushed at Holten. Eli dodged the deadly blade and butt-stroked the mercenary. The satisfying crunch of jawbone transmitted up Holten's arms.

Gagging on his blood, the freebooter staggered three steps away, to have his head split top to bottom by the handaxe of a Yaqui warrior. Steadily, with deadly accuracy, the riflemen beyond the camp kept up covering fire while those inside closed in vicious hand-to-hand fighting. Eli reached the place where Carlos crouched behind a small hand cart that provided scant cover.

"There . . . see what I mean?"

Holten looked along the path of Ocampo's pointing finger. Some of the mercenaries had constructed a makeshift barricade of collapsed tents, shoulder packs and corpses. They knelt behind it and unleashed withering volleys that scythed through the brave Yaquis and peons attempting to rush the crude fortification.

"We need a little help. Those *cabrónes* have us in a real fix, no?"

"One of these might help." Holten reached into his saddle bags while he spoke.

From it he extracted a small, spherical clay object. A fuse protruded from a tiny hole in its top. Inside, the scout knew, was a collection of broken, rusty nails, bits of jagged iron and a pound of blasting powder. For good measure, he brought out a second grenade. While the mercenaries continued to rake the area with well-aimed gunfire, Eli pulled a cigar from his pocket, bit off the end and lighted it with a lucifer. Then he ignited the fuse, watched until it burned freely, rose and hurled it toward the barricade.

In the scant firelight, it disappeared quickly, only a trailing wake of orange sparks to mark its flight. Already, Eli bent to retrieve the second hand bomb and give life to its fuse. A moment later the first one exploded behind the bulwark of camp gear. Screams and howls of agony followed.

Holten hurled the second explosive package.

It, too, brought shrieks of pain and a misty splash of blood.

"You did it!" Carlos exalted. "That fixed them."

Carlos rose and started to wave his peon soldiers onward. Then a loud blast sounded to the left and he sprayed his blood and brains all over Eli Holten's head and shoulders.

Grief and rage warred in the scout's mind. "Carlos!" he shouted, knowing it did no good.

Eli grabbed for his Winchester when a commanding voice spoke out of the cloud of powder smoke.

"Don't even try it."

Milo Madonna stepped closer, into view, a smoking rifle to his shoulder, the muzzle centered on the scout's forehead.

Chapter 24

Eli Holten had fought worthier opponents. Never, though, had he encountered an enemy who seemed so much in control. One who had the strength and ability to use his unusual talents properly to stay on top.

The thoughts came to him in an eye-blink of time, while he crouched on the ground, two feet from his Winchester. The Winchester in Iron Mike's hands never wavered. Around them the fury of battle continued, ebbing to one side, then the other. Madonna took another step toward him.

One more, you son of a bitch, the scout willed with all his concentrated mindforce. The cigar still smoldered in one corner of his mouth. Holten made a face that reflected distaste. An easy task, with part of the contents of Carlos' skull still dripping from his brow ridge.

"The cigar," he croaked. "Mind if I take it out? Don't taste too good, mixed with blood."

A flicker of smile animated Madonna's features. "Go ahead. I smoke the same kind myself, so I know what you mean. Do it slowly. Right hand."

With exaggerated slowness, the scout reached across his face to remove the cigar. As he did, his body now turned partly away from Madonna, his left hand crept backward. He pulled the stogie from his lips and rolled it between his thumb and middle finger. Holten forced a smile and looked up toward his captor.

Madonna nodded, pleased with the cooperation.

Then Eli flicked his fingers forward and the burning tip of his cigar arched over the short distance. It struck Milo Madonna under the left eye.

Madonna gasped at the sudden pain and his vision blurred as tears formed. In the same instant, Holten's left arm came forward. He clinched his Bowie tightly in big fingers, as he dived toward his enemy's legs.

Taken off guard, his face smarting with pain, involuntary tears still blinding his eyes, Madonna took a stumbling step backward. Awkwardly, he tried to get lined up for a clear shot.

Holten's blade flashed as he swung it. The keen edge sliced easily through heavy trouser material and bit deeply into Madonna's right calf. The big mercenary's rifle exploded over the scout's head and Holten felt the powerful wind of the bullet's passage. Burning bits of powder stung Eli's exposed neck and ears. He ignored it, and the odor of burning hair, to lunge again as Madonna crashed to the ground.

Severely injured, but undaunted, Iron Mike Madonna rolled away from the deadly threat of the dripping blade. He swung his Winchester like a club and smashed the buttstock solidly into the point of Eli's left shoulder.

Pain messages screamed along Holten's nerves. Undirected, his fingers flexed a fraction of a second and the knife fell from his hand. Eli looked up to see a big boot headed directly for his face. He leaped up and backward, stumbling over Carlos Ocampo's corpse. Iron Mike crawled after him.

"You're good," the mercenary captain panted. "You must be Eli Holten."

"I am," is all the scout allowed.

"Connie told me about you." With each labored word, Madonna pulled himself closer to the scout. He swung the rifle again, then reversed it so his finger curled around the trigger.

"Connie is a bitch."

To the scout's surprise, Madonna didn't fire. Instead, he threw back his head and laughed heartily. "How's that old saying go? 'Yeah, but she's *my* bitch.' You should have been with us."

"I enjoyed being against you."

"Hard, Holten. You're one hard son of a bitch."

Up on hands and knees, Holten maneuvered toward his own rifle. Blood seeped steadily from Milo Madonna's cut calf. Every second weakened the mercenary. Explosions ripped the night air and the keening cries of the injured told Eli Holten that José Descalso had finished with the cannons and started in with his grenades. Swaying silhouettes, locked in mortal combat, flickered at the edges of his vision. Eli's seeking hand closed on the forestock of his Model '73.

"Of course, you have to be," Madonna continued talking as the pair changed position, each angling for his own advantage. "Henshaw was no tactical genius, but to defeat him and some forty mutineers took a lot of balls."

"Thank you."

Holten had his Winchester in hand now, his back angled toward Madonna. He mentally counted to four and turned rapidly.

Both rifles vomited flame and smoke at the same instant.

Madonna's bullet plowed into Holten's right shoulder. Impact sent the scout's Winchester flying. His own slug, though, had already left the barrel.

A look of dull surprise washed over Milo Madonna's face. Hot lead, from Eli Holten's .44-40 had entered his body through his groin. It lanced hotly up the length of his body and then, robbed of most of its momentum, it failed to exit entirely, which left a conical bulge in the skin between his collar bone and left shoulder blade.

Holten came to his knees, his six-gun ready in his left hand. Milo Madonna feebly waved at him in resignation and coughed. A trickle of blood preceded his words.

"I . . . I'm done for." A ghost of Iron Mike's former bright smile lighted his pain-ravaged face. "Anyhow . . . it was . . . one hell of a fight, Holten, you hard son of a bitch."

Milo Madonna gave a mighty shudder and offered up his spirit.

Weak from wounds and exertion, Eli Holten rose to his feet. He swayed like a drunken man, somewhat foggy vision wavering as he looked around him. Everywhere his gaze passed, members of the free company went down fighting rather than endure capture. All organized resistance had crumbled. Holten sucked great gulps of cool night air into his punished lungs and bellowed at the top of his voice.

"Iron Mike Madonna is dead. Give up and I promise you that you will not be tortured or disfigured. Surrender now or die to the last man."

Slowly, the survivors began to capitulate. Weaving,

only now giving in to his grief at the loss of a good friend, Eli Holten started a necessary search. Half an hour later, he had to admit it had happened again.

Nowhere did he find any trace of Constance Williams.

High up on the narrow trail that led to the continuation of the road to La Paz, Constance Williams paused and looked back at the now-silent camp below. She felt dizzy, frightened of a misstep. Her breath came in gasping sobs, while tears lined her cheeks. At last she drew a deep breath and shook her fist at the distant, ant-like figures who rampaged through the ruins.

"Some day. Some day I'll get you," she vowed. Then, unknowingly, she repeated Milo Madonna's final words. "Eli Holten, you hard son of a bitch!"

THE SURVIVALIST SERIES
by Jerry Ahern

#1: TOTAL WAR	(0960, $2.50)
#2: THE NIGHTMARE BEGINS	(0810, $2.50)
#3: THE QUEST	(0851, $2.50)
#4: THE DOOMSAYER	(0893, $2.50)
#5: THE WEB	(1145, $2.50)
#6: THE SAVAGE HORDE	(1232, $2.50)
#7: THE PROPHET	(1339, $2.50)
#8: THE END IS COMING	(1374, $2.50)
#9: EARTH FIRE	(1405, $2.50)
#10: THE AWAKENING	(1478, $2.50)
#11: THE REPRISAL	(1590, $2.50)
#12: THE REBELLION	(1676, $2.50)